THE GIFT AT THE SPRINGHOUSE

BY

JEANNE LEFEVRE

INFINITY
PUBLISHING

ISBN 978-0-7414-5936-7

Printed in the United States of America

This is a work of fiction. Names, characters, places, and incidents either are the product of the author's imagination or are used fictitiously. Any resemblance to actual events or locales or persons, living or dead, is entirely coincidental.

Published November 2012

INFINITY PUBLISHING

Toll-free (877) BUY BOOK
Local Phone (610) 941-9999
Fax (610) 941-9959
Info@buybooksontheweb.com
www.buybooksontheweb.com

DEDICATED TO MY FAMILY

Many thanks to the people in my community who have given me the ideas and images for this book, and the privilege to write about their inspiring contributions.

Jeff LeFevre

Jill and Scott Burns - Photography

Tom Dengler

Pat Mickowski

Phyllis Bechtel

Janice Hofmann

Eunice Buskirk

Nancy Satow

Henry Smith

Louise Bechtel

Bob and Linda Hetrick

Donald and Ginny Haydt

Alan and Debbie Boyer
owners of the Springhouse

Gary and Marcia Burns
owners of the Honeymoon Hideaway

Rob and Elizabeth Price
owners of Hersch's market

Robin Miah and Steve Durgan
owners of Slatington Diner

Table of Contents

Gram's House

Gram's Rocker

Prologue

The day was perfect for the celebration. It was early April, and spring was slowly guiding the earth out of its winter hibernation. Friends from the community seated themselves on the chairs under the budding hickory and walnut trees in the front yard of her old Victorian home. The modest front porch, crowned with gingerbread lattice when it was built in 1860, was decorated with grapevine and burgundy ribbons for this special occasion. A clay pot filled with rosemary sat on the right side of the front door. It was the perfect setting for today's guest of honor.

A small, gray haired woman sat on a green, wooden, rocking chair. She wore a black suit with a round, black, velvet hat slanted fashionably on the right side of her head, and secured with a pearl hat pin. A corsage of white baby roses, pinned to her lapel, complimented her grandmother's white pearls that she wore around her neck. The scent of Chantilly surrounded her. Next to her, a tall, thin gentleman, dressed in a black formal suit and a top hat, stood behind a homemade podium.

"Good day to everyone," he began. "It is good to see all of you here today at the home of our dear friend, Tess."

The people in front of her all smiled and applauded.

"We know her as a writer, a journalist, and an author," he continued, "but most important, we celebrate her today as a teacher, a caretaker, and a friend to all of us that ever needed her. Tess is a true pillar of our community, who we highly respect and admire. Today, we will present her with a very special award. We like to call it the Noble Prize of Hopewell. We award it to an individual who has shown outstanding dedication to our community, and a selfless giving of oneself to our people, our animals, our town, and our environment. Each year, the townspeople vote on who should receive this honor. This year, Tess has unanimously won our vote. On behalf of our little town, I take great pride in presenting her with this honor on her 100th birthday."

When the people finished applauding, the mayor turned to Tess to help her up from the rocker. Slowly, she placed her wooden cane in front of her and steadied herself up and onto her feet. Then she took a few steps until she stood right behind the podium.

"Thank you, thank you," she said, as her voice trembled, and her eyes filled with tears.

All rose from their seats for a standing ovation.

"Please, sit down. Please, take your seats," she motioned, patting her quivering hand gently on the stand in front of her. Everyone became seated.

"I am so happy to see all of you," she began. "For many years, I have sat where you are today and covered this event for our newspaper. In the past, I have written stories about so many of the extraordinary heroes that received this award, I see that I have ultimately been mistaken for one of them today."

They applauded. She bowed her head for a moment, regained her composure, and looked straight ahead at her audience.

"I thank all of you from the bottom of my heart," she continued.

Again, her listeners clapped. Tess tapped the podium for a second time, and everyone became quiet around her. She repositioned herself with the help of her cane, and as she resumed speaking, a bright red cardinal positioned himself on a branch of the old shag bark hickory, and a red-tailed hawk began circling above the house.

"Since I am a storyteller at heart," she said, "I am going to tell you all a story on this beautiful, sunny afternoon. I would be remiss if I accepted this award without giving the credit to those who truly made it possible. I stand here today because of all the extraordinary people that I have met along the way, especially one who loved me so much that she allowed me to stand on her shoulders, in my defining moments, so I could see beyond my limited vision. She is the real hero of the day, and I simply remain the vessel of her life and her life story."

She paused as if holding back her tears. Then she continued.

"My dear friends, I invite you to listen with an open heart to this powerful and compelling tale that I am about to share with you. There are those of you who will believe this story without question. For you, it is complete, and there is no further explanation necessary. However, there are others at this time who will find it simply unbelievable. For those, please understand that there is no further explanation possible. Regardless, I love you all so much, and I thank you for granting me this great honor today."

The crowd applauded passionately. Tess took a moment and gazed at all the people in front of her. She closed her eyes for a second as if she were memorizing the picture in front of her. Then she steadied herself and slowly turned away from the podium.

Returning to her rocker, she made herself comfortable. She opened up her worn journal, cleared her voice, and began to tell her story.

"Many, many years and a thousand miles ago..."

Day One

It was a cold, early March evening when I reached the unpaved, abandoned road that led to her old farm. The drive to my Gram's house seemed to take forever. On a typical day, I was there in less than a half hour, but the distance from the cemetery, Gram's final physical resting place, to my early childhood home seemed to take longer than usual today.

The scenery on the way was the same as always. Easing around the bend and heading north, I could see the snow covered hill dotted with homes that always reminded my Gram of a small village in Germany. Although she lived in Pennsylvania all of her life and never traveled to that country, in her mind's eye, she believed that was exactly the way it looked. Many times when I would go home to see her, she would comment on the hillside on our way back from our shopping trips.

As the years ran quickly by, so did I. The visits home and the shopping trips became less and less. She grew older tending to the farm, and I grew busier in New England pursuing academic degrees. After graduating from Boston College, I quickly settled into my new life, and my fascinating and advancing career in journalism.

I traveled these roads a hundred times as a child, a young girl, then as a grown woman, always with the anticipation that Gram would be there to welcome me when I arrived home. When she heard the car coming up the road, she would be standing there as I opened the car door. Smiling, she would cup her two hands around my face, take one moment to look at me, and then give me the kiss that only she could give. I felt disappointed that today I would not feel her touch or receive a gentle kiss.

Today would be different than any of my other visits home.

The Lane to Gram's House

After bearing the car to the left and coasting down the hill into the hollow, I reached the stone mill on the right. Slowing the car down around the curve, I made a left turn onto the unpaved road, passed Gram's mailbox, and I headed for the old Victorian farmhouse straight ahead. A light snow was starting to fall. The old wooden rocking chairs on the front porch were moving back and forth, being persuaded by the same northeast wind that was inviting the falling snowflakes to dance in a random style. At first, I thought I saw my Gram seated on one of the green rockers, but with a blink of an eye, and a second glance, the image quickly disappeared.

As usual, I parked my car in front of the stone barn and turned off the ignition. The snow, no longer feeling the need to obey the wiper, began to settle on the windshield for the night. The deer were in the field straight ahead, most likely searching for their last meal of the day. If it were one hour later, I would only recognize them by the shiny dots that represented their eyes, as the headlights came to rest upon them.

The cold, brisk wind brushed against my face when I got out of the car. The evening air always smelled so fresh and crisp at Gram's farm. I crossed the road and made my way up the three cement steps. It was heartbreaking to return to her house alone tonight, only to find her memory in the stone path leading to her back door. A clay pot of dried, frozen rosemary rested on its side next to it. The bird feeder was empty with only a few determined birds looking for the left over seed that fell on the ground. The summer kitchen stood straight ahead, and I could see that this year Gram did not seal the windows with black plastic to keep out the cold wind and snow. She always made sure this was done before the winter arrived. This year, I thought that Gram may have felt too weak to do the job, but for a moment I wondered if that was really the case.

The Window of the Summer Kitchen

Perhaps Gram knew that I would be returning alone this time of year, for as the wind whistled through the broken glass, it sounded as if an old raspy voice was welcoming me home. I pulled the wooden screen door toward me, and it let out with a squeak. As always, the key fit snugly into the brass lock, but the deadbolt, to my surprise, was already released, and the door opened with a slight twist of the knob. Gram must have forgotten to have the door secured when she left in the ambulance, I thought. Her call to the hospital was urgent, since the nagging pain in her chest was getting worse, and she was hoping for some relief. I quickly dismissed any other reason for the door being open. The house was quiet and still, and even though I was comfortable continuing on my way in the dark, I knew I would feel more at ease if I turned on some lights. Taking a few steps into the kitchen, I reached for the switch on the wall, and immediately the dim lamp above the sink provided me with the amount of light that I needed.

It was good to be here. I always loved when I came home and stepped into Gram's kitchen. It smelled so delicious and felt so inviting, just like when I lived here. I tried to imitate what she did to make it that way. After putting the kettle on for tea, I shoveled some coal into the old, gray stove that stood in the brick alcove. Gram always had the coal bucket full of coal and ready to go. She taught me how to build a fire when I was old enough, and I had to practice until I could do it correctly. Following her same instructions tonight, I was able to get the stove started and just about the time the teapot whistled, the first, blue, dancing flame was peeking through the black layer of coals.

Gram always stored her loose Chamomile tea leaves in a glass jar in the wooden cupboard, but tonight the jar was sitting next to Gram's favorite china tea cup on a small table alongside the stove. Seeping the leaves, I sat down at the kitchen table to enjoy some of my delicious and calming tea. That was one of the first things we would do when I came to visit. Gram made the tea, and we would sit down to talk. She wanted to hear about everything that I was doing. She was excited to hear about my latest achievements and willing to listen to all of my problems. Always so loving and caring throughout the conversation, she would take my hand and tell me that she was incredibly proud of me. Although tonight I was sitting here alone, I could not help but feel her presence surrounding me.

I had planned to stay a week or two packing Gram's things and getting the house in order for its upcoming sale. I wanted to sit here tonight and take some time to organize the week ahead, but I felt exhausted all of a sudden. Even though it was still early for sleep, the events from the funeral today, the warmth of the fire, the soothing tea, and the thought of snow blanketing the house, persuaded me to retire and start my chores in the morning.

Making my way up the narrow set of stairs, I walked into Gram's bedroom. I wanted to sleep in her room tonight, so I could benefit from the heat that was slowly inching its way up to the second floor. I turned on the crystal lamp sitting on her dresser. Since my bags were still in the car, I began to look for one of Gram's night gowns until I could unpack my own clothing in the morning. I did not have to look very far, for on the dark green divan there lay a folded, pink night gown, as if it were placed there and waiting for me. Thrilled that I did not have to search for one, I dressed for bed, climbed under the large down comforter that lay across her iron bed, and snuggled well into its warmth.

As a child, my mother and I would recite prayers at bedtime. She taught me a simple prayer like, 'Now I Lay Me Down to Sleep' as well as others that I committed to memory.

As I grew older, Gram showed me a different way to pray.

At night, just before I went to sleep, Gram taught me to think about my day, and give thanks to God for all the blessings I received, both seen and unseen. She taught me to forgive myself for my mistakes, or for making some decisions that were not the best.

Gram's Divan

I'd ask forgiveness from those that I may have offended and ask for help to do things a little better. Then I would say a homemade prayer that she taught me and ask God to give me just what I needed, nothing more or nothing less. Before Gram left my room, she would kiss me and say, 'good night, sleep tight, and see you in the morning light.'

Lying in Gram's bed tonight and thinking about her, I suddenly realized that I had become so absorbed in my own success that I had forgotten how to pray. For a second, I felt ashamed that I neglected to see past my own dazzling life, and give thanks to anyone but myself.

All of a sudden, I had a desire to search for the peace that I use to feel when I lived here. I desperately wanted to try to remember the prayer Gram taught me as a little girl. For some odd reason, when I finally began to recite the words, I heard another voice whispering something different. Mine became still, and my Gram's voice became louder, as I heard her say.

The world is full wonder, each time a new sun breaks
It leaves us with a story, as the moon and owl awake
The story is a message, for the open heart to take
The world is full wonder, each time a new sun breaks

Unable to conclude what I did not understand, I attempted to release the fear of the unknown and embrace the comfort of sleep.

13

Day Two

I woke up to the six chimes of the grandfather clock that was downstairs in Gram's parlor. It seemed to peacefully call the morning in compared to the loud, buzzing alarm clock that woke me up every day in Boston. It was still dark outside and, for a moment, I forgot where I was. When I realized that I was at Gram's house, I became very comfortable and somewhat reflective. What a marvelous room this is, I thought, as I lay in bed still snuggled and warm under the down comforter.

My grandmother, Angeline, was born in this very room. As Gram tells the story, her mother, Mary, asked her husband, Charles, to 'go get the doctor' from the town because she was about to give birth to their baby. He became so excited that he ran out of the house and down the lane until he realized that his Model T, parked by the barn, would certainly get him there and back faster than his legs could take him.

"The doctor arrived just in time to welcome me into the world on October 10, 1913," Gram said.
She told me that her mother would feed and comfort her on a rocking chair that was next to the window overlooking their fruit orchard. When she fell asleep, her mother placed her in the white, spindled crib where her old iron bed now stands.

I felt honored waking up in such an incredible room. A tea stained wallpaper, dotted with tiny pink and green flowers, covered the plastered walls. Rose colored trim framed the doors and windows, and a matching crown molding bordered the entire room. Delicate lace curtains hung on all four windows that were supported by thick, deep sills. A charming stone fireplace rested against the west wall. On the mantle were oval framed pictures of Gram's mother and father, and my mother and father.
In the corner there was a worn green divan. It was here that we would sit, and Gram would tell me stories about her

14

mother and father, and her brother, Vincent. Gram's parents loved and cared for their family and farmed the one hundred and fifty acres that surrounded the farmhouse.

It was Gram's great-great grandparents, Patrizia and Antonio Tamarazzo, who sailed from Calabria, Italy, and bought land from Antonio's brother, Carmen when they got married in 1836. At first, they built and lived in a small log cabin with the name, 'honeymoon hideout,' crudely carved above the front door. The structure still stands in a clearing on this land, close to the old Springhouse. They built the barn in 1838 and the summer kitchen in 1840. They lived in the summer kitchen until they completed this house in 1860. She told me that the house was built in this exact location for several reasons. They wanted the front of the house to be the first place that welcomed the sun as it came over the horizon, and rose to its glory in the morning sky. The back of the house was built close to the hill to protect it from the harsh, northeast wind and storms. When Patrizia and Antonio died, the house went to their only living son, Bruno, and his wife, Millie. Then their oldest son, Mauro, and his wife, Alvita, eventually inherited it. When Mauro and Alvita died, the land went to their favorite son, Charles and his new bride, Mary, who were my great grandparents. Gram and my grandfather, Peter, lived with Gram's parents and helped them farm the land. Vincent died from polio shortly after Gram's parents died, and so Gram became the sole owner of the homestead.

My mother, Anna Gia, was also born in this house on March 14, 1933. She was their only child. She married my father, James Vincenzo Orlando, on September 27, 1951, and I came into the world on April 9, 1953, in the small, local hospital in Hopewell, Pennsylvania.

My mother and father lived with my grandparents until I was born. Shortly after that, my father, a teacher by profession, acquired a job in a high school in Abington, Pennsylvania. We left Grams and moved into a quaint gray and white house on Main Street, near the school.

Patrizia Tamarazzo

The Honeymoon Hideout

We lived there for about eight years, and we returned to the farm every summer when school was out to help with the farming.

One day, my father took the train into Philadelphia on some business, and he was killed in a tragic accident as the train was returning to Abington. My mother, very lonely and unable to support us in the city, moved us back to Gram's farm when I was eight. I remember that we had to leave some of our things behind because Gram did not have enough room to store all of our belongings. I remember pleading with my mother to take along my little rocking chair that I loved, even though I was too tall to sit in it. After quite a bit of crying, my mother finally gave in, but she said that we would have to keep it in Gram's attic. I agreed and carried that little chair to the car myself. When we got to Gram's, I carried it up the steps, and into the house. I always found comfort in that little rocker, especially after my mother died two years later from pneumonia. Gram moved the chair into my new bedroom that was now next to theirs. From that day on, Gram and Gramps became everything to me, and this wonderful farm became my home.

As Gram's executor and only heir, I knew that one day I would own my childhood home. Now at fifty-six, it belonged to me, along with my decision to sell it. There was no doubt in my mind, I planned to return to Boston. My life in New England as a renowned journalist, and a prominent writer was, although busy, very rewarding. My assignments took me throughout the world covering news events and leading documentaries. I loved my lifestyle there. Although I never married, I enjoyed my single life, and I afforded myself a relatively affluent standard of living. I had influential friends in the city, and indulged in the luxuries that I wanted. My stay on Gram's farm would be short. With that in mind, I wanted to get started with the matter at hand.

The first thing I needed to do was dress, eat breakfast, and then pick up Jake, Gram's chocolate Labrador. Mrs. Como, Gram's neighbor and friend, who owned the farm down the road, looked after Jake at her place while Gram was home recuperating from her hospital stay. I called her this morning and asked if I could stop by and pick up Jake today. I also wanted to know if she wanted any of Gram's things.

"I hope you can stay and visit awhile, Tess, I would love to have some time to talk with you," she said on the phone.

Gram knew Carmella a long time, ever since Carmella married Ray Como and moved to the farm down the road. Gram baked a cake, and she and Gramps carried it to the Como's home to congratulate them, and particularly to give his new bride a warm welcome to the community. She was Gram's good friend, and I believe they became dearest friends after Ray and Gramps died from heart problems within two years of each other.

I remember, back then, Gram and I would take walks every Sunday afternoon to visit with Mrs. Como. I always loved going to her house. When we got there, the kitchen table was set with a lace tablecloth, lovely tea cups and saucers, and a green tinted milk glass for me. She would have a plate of fresh baked butter cookies waiting for us along with a bowl of strawberries, and a dish of chocolates. Her arms would be wide open to greet us. Without a doubt, I thought, even though my day will be busy, I must make time to stay and visit with her today.

Carrying the suitcases from the car to the house was tricky this morning. It snowed all night, and toward the end of the storm, it turned from snow to ice. Living in New England, I was terribly familiar with the cold, northeast winters and icy chill, and so I was well equipped with my down coat, and ice breakers for my boots. Safely in the house again, I showered, dressed, and made my way back to the car. I was heading to Charlie's diner, 7 miles away in the little town of Hopewell, population, 2,106.

Every Saturday, Gramps would treat Gram and me to breakfast at Charlie's. If I could remember correctly, Charlie was the cook and made the best breakfast in town.

Charlie's Diner

Ellie, our favorite waitress at the diner, always waited on our table and would ask Gramps the same question.

"What will you be having today, Pete? Will it be eggs with bacon, or bacon with eggs?"

"Yep," he answered, looking directly at her and smiling.

Those were glorious times, I thought. As an unfamiliar face walked up to my table and took my order, I realized how quickly the years slipped away. Sipping my coffee, I took a journal out of my purse and started to take some notes. I wanted to continue documenting this trip until I returned to Boston. If all went as planned, I could turn my stay here into my fourth book. I would create an incredible story about my childhood years, and other memories of the farm. The ending would be powerful, as I prepared to place the old homestead into the hands of a new owner. Yes, this story should put me on the best-seller list again.

For as long as I could remember, I loved to read and write. Gram always read to me when I was young until I learned, then she would ask me to read to her. By the time I was ten, I was making up tales of my own. Although Gram and I use to sit on the front porch and read, our favorite spot to tell stories to one another was at the Springhouse. We would sit there together at dusk and make up tales that sometimes even scared us.

When I went to high school, I found part time work doing odd jobs at our local newspaper, the Hopewell Chronicle. It gave me an opportunity to hang around the people that wrote the news and other sensational stories about our little town, and the people that lived there. I think that is where my passion for the written word all started. They inspired me and fanned the flame of the writer in me. By the time I graduated from high school, I decided that I wanted a career in journalism.

Quickly jotting down some notes about the diner, I noticed that things looked almost the same. The silver and red counter, and the matching bar stools were still located on the right side and ran almost the whole length of the diner. It was an open invitation to the town folk to come in, sit down, and get their morning eye opener. That included a strong, hot cup of coffee, some serious debate, a lively conversation, and the day's news provided by at least two free counter copies of the local newspaper. The morning regulars had their own coffee mugs that sat on a wooden shelf next to the coffee urn. Charlie or Ellie would have the coffee poured and waiting on the counter as they saw the cup's owner coming through the door. Charlie, being the short-order cook, would always join in the community chatter, as he fried the bacon and sausage and flipped or scrambled the eggs on the grill directly behind him. They discussed everything from farm prices and local elections, to factory problems and road conditions. Ellie would wait on the customers that occupied the tan and red booths. She never wrote any of the orders down, rather yelled them out to Charlie, as she went from table to table. It always amazed me how he could cook, talk to the locals, and, ten out of ten times, get the orders right. In between serving the customers, Ellie prepared fresh pots of coffee, cleared the dishes, and wiped the tables with the same white and green square cloth that she rinsed out several times.

Charlie passed on a few years ago, and his son, Bob, took over. The diner still had a relaxed atmosphere, but there were some changes. Small matching coffee cups were now used, leaving the faithful old mugs as cherished trophies to the loyal customers that once used them. The waitresses wore black pants and white blouses instead of pink uniforms with matching aprons and crowns.

The small, individual 'No Smoking' signs that matched the larger one that hung above the glass pie case behind the counter, replaced the artificial flowers on the tables. Unlike Charlie, Bob didn't do the cooking, so depending on the day, a new face could be seen at the grill.

Charlie's Diner

I put the journal on the table as I saw the smiling waitress heading toward my table while balancing a tray full of food. The dish bearing the bacon, eggs, home fries, and toast was mine. Also approaching my table from another direction, was an elderly woman, who I immediately recognized as an older looking Ellie.

"Hello, Darling," she said.

"Hello, Ellie," I replied, getting up from my chair to give her a hug.

"Sorry I could not make the funeral yesterday, but it was so cold, and that terribly painful arthritis just would not let me be," she said, leaning on her cane and trying to return the hug the best way she possibly could.

"Please, sit down and join me, Ellie," I said.

As soon as she sat down, a cup and saucer and a pot of hot tea arrived at the table for her.

"That young one tries to outdo the service I gave to people when I worked here. Did you know that I trained her mother at waitressing? I guess the good old lessons about knowing your customers and keeping them happy got handed down," Ellie said with a smile. "Anyway, it is good to see you, Tess. I imagine we will be seeing a lot more of you when you move back to the farm. Your grandmother always took great pride in that place, especially since it was in her family for generations. It was a real jewel to her, just like you. When do you think you will be moving back?" Ellie inquired.

It surprised me that Ellie thought I would be returning to Hopewell. After all, Gram must have told her about my popularity and success in New England.

"I will not be keeping the farm, Ellie," I said. "As soon as I can get it ready for sale, I will be putting it on the market, and I will be returning to Boston."

"Oh, I am so sorry dear," Ellie said, "I just took for granted that you were coming back to the homestead. I guess all of us that have lived and worked in Hopewell all of our lives feel a deep affection for our beloved little town. We think everyone should feel the same way about being here.

Well, Tess, we do not know what tomorrow has in store for us, but as long as we can measure our life by the good we do for others, I guess it doesn't matter where we are."

With that, she adjusted her hat, raised herself on the cane that steadied her, gently kissed me on the forehead, and excused herself. When I looked out the window, I could see Ellie boarding the bus that would take her back to her home on the outskirts of town.

As I sat there finishing my breakfast, I could not help but have mixed feelings about my conversation with Ellie. It was sure delightful to see her, but wherever did she get the notion that I would be coming back to live on a farm? Gram lived in Hopewell all of her life, and I vowed it would be different with me, I thought. Gram always taught me to choose my own future, and I left this town in the hopes of becoming successful in a field other than nursing, teaching, or farming. In my own defense, I did not believe that my fate should be handed down to me. I did not have to become my mother, or my mother's mother. I may have inherited their eyes, hips, and face, but that did not mean that I had to inherit their fate. I did not have to live the same lives as the women who came before me.

Suddenly, as silly as that seemed, I continued arguing with myself.

After all, I thought, my fate is not like a favorite hat that my Gram wore, and then passed down for my mom to wear, and now for me to wear. What do I do with it if it doesn't fit me? How do I know that it is the right one for me? Years ago, I had an opportunity to try on a brand new hat, and, as it turns out, it fits me a lot better than the one handed down. Nobody else should be the judge of what is right for me. Yes, journalism in Boston suits me a lot better than farming in Hopewell.

As I left the diner, the sound of muffled voices engaged in conversation followed me to the door. Standing on the sidewalk and looking up and down the street, I immediately missed the days gone by. These people touched my life, and

I left them behind. Suddenly, I longed not only for my Gram and Gramps, but, oddly enough, I longed for Charlie and Ellie too.

My next stop was to Mrs. Como's house. I wanted to visit with her and pick up Gram's loyal friend, Jake. She was waiting at the door when she heard the car pull up alongside the house. Jake started to bark. Thank God some things never change, I thought. Folks around here know what the word 'welcome' means. They greet you at the door when you arrive. In Boston, the door is a protective shield that is not opened until some identification is made on one side of it, and accepted on the other.

"Hi, Mrs. Como," I said.

We gave each other a hug. Carmela was almost ninety, but her petite frame, her barely gray hair, and her fair skin that revealed very few wrinkles, challenged her chronological age. She wore a homemade blue and yellow flowered house dress covered by a solid blue apron. I could smell the Chantilly perfume from where I was standing.

"Come in, come in," she said, "we have been waiting for you."

Jake nuzzled his nose under my arm, hoping to get a pat on the head and some attention.

"He has been a good boy for me, but I could tell that he misses Angeline, as we all do."

When I entered, I recognized the familiar scent of mild cedar and patchouli. It was like stepping into her parlor when I was a child. While I stood there, the time between little girl and grown women became blurred, as the memories flooded in and became impatient to be recalled. Both of us loved Gram so much, and together we were an unlimited source of Gram's remembrances, gestures, expressions, and dreams.

Jake

"Now come and sit down while I warm the tea, and we can visit for a while," she said.

There were two cups sitting on the table, along with all the goodies. Although she had slowed down a little, from what I could tell, her energy had not diminished very much. She returned to the table with the tea and, as always, made sure I was comfortable. Jake took his position at her feet in the hopes of being offered a small snack.

"That was a beautiful ceremony and lovely reception you had for your Gram yesterday," Mrs. Como said. "You know, she always loved the late summer and fall. She wanted to pass on in the winter when her favorite time of the year was over. I'd say that her timing was pretty good."

Gram was ninety-nine when she died, and she had requested a few things that she wanted upon her death. Gram's body was taken in an oak casket from the funeral parlor in Hopewell to the old, red brick Unity Church by a horse drawn hearse. The two hefty, large horses, donning black feathered headdresses, pulled a black coach that rolled on four large, thin wheels. The sides of the enclosed coach were made of glass, and Gram's name was written across the center. On the wooden seat up front, there were two men dressed in black coat tails and top hats holding the reins and driving the horses. They took the back road that passed Gram's farm on the way to the church, just as she wished.

The church was filled with people that knew Gram. She had a few close friends that were still alive, but I think most of the town folks, young and old, considered her their friend. Although she belonged to the church, my Gram followed her own spirituality. She did not believe that God was this untouchable, judgmental, being that sat on a throne in heaven. She believed that God was the Power to exist, and the Highest Good. She believed that He was the nature that surrounded her, and the people that she met every day. My Gram was the most loving and kindest person I had ever known. The two verses she requested, 'The Lord is my Shepherd' and 'The Lord's Prayer' were read by the minister, and the poem, 'Do not stand by my Grave and Weep' was recited. They sung her favorite songs, 'How Great Thou Art,' and 'It's a Wonderful World.' Both were done beautifully by the members of the choir. After the service, her body was cremated, and her ashes were returned to the church cemetery for burial.

The cemetery where Gram was laid to rest was behind the Unity church. The spires looked as if they reached all the way up to heaven, and they were illuminated at night along with the bell tower. It was one of Gram's favorite sights. If we were passing the church at dusk, she would ask me to pull alongside the road. She would gaze at the church and listen to the bells. Now, most of her remains were buried right there, except for a small amount of her ashes that were placed into a walnut box and taken back to the farm. She requested in her Last Will and Testament that I spread the rest of her ashes at the Springhouse, specifically around the bench that Gramps made for her. It was one of her favorite places to relax and, I believe, pray. Many times we would sit there on a hot, summer afternoon and refresh ourselves with a glass of cool water that flowed from the spring. In the fall, we sat on the bench and watched October host its annual party, as beautiful leaves of every color fell to the ground. Gram loved the time of year when the earth prepared for winter. There was a natural desire to clear out the old, and prepare for the new. A subtle but definite shift in energy could be felt. Gram always honored the change of seasons.

Yes, I would follow her wishes before I returned to Boston.

"You know, Tess, I think Angeline knew that she was not going to get better," Carmela said.

"I think you are right, Mrs. Como," I replied, as my thoughts drifted back to the time Gram became ill.

Over the last two months, Gram had been in and out of the hospital three times, and I stayed with her as much as I could. When I thought she was getting stronger, I drove to Boston for two days to take care of some of my business. The day I was returning to her, she had the sudden heart attack. I received the call from the doctor that she was in critical condition, and I drove straight to the hospital to be with her.

She looked so calm as I sat by her bedside. She would often tell me that when she used up all the heartbeats that God had given to her, she would be willing to go with Him. She had no fear of dying.

"I believe that it is one of the most extraordinary moments for us, Tess, when our body dissolves and our spirit is called Home. It is a watchful time, and the final journey for the soul, as it seamlessly returns to the Oneness from where it came. Whether you believe Heaven is a place in the sky, or deep inside your soul," she would say, "it is a place of complete and total peace and happiness."

She believed that it was important to be as aware as one can be at that moment, and she was. Her room was quiet with only a dim light on above the bed. She was lying on her back with her eyes closed and her hands folded. The intravenous tube was connected to her left hand, and the heart monitor was placed across her chest. When I knelt down beside her bed, she turned her head toward me, and I took her hand in mine.

"Tess," she whispered.

"Yes, Gram, I'm here."

"Tess, please pray with me."

She started reciting 'The Lord's Prayer.' I began to cry as I started to pray with her. She squeezed my hand and slowly released it. The monitors sounded their alarms, and the nurses and doctor ran into the room. Nothing was done since Gram requested that no life-saving measures be performed. I looked at Gram, and she looked so peaceful. One moment she was conscious and here, and in an instant, she was lifeless and There. I believe Gram knew her time was close, even though she was feeling better. She encouraged me to go back to my job, and told me that if I did not continue on with my work, her illness would take two lives instead of one. She promised me that she would not leave this earth until I came back. Carmela wanted to stay with her, but she insisted that she also go home, promising that she would call if she needed her. Gram was always an extremely private person, and I believe that she needed the time alone with her God to prepare for her departure from this world, and her arrival into the next.

"We are all given a journey," she would tell us, "and when our work is done, there is no reason for us to stay on this earth. We are not here one moment longer than we are supposed to be. When it is our time, Tess, some illness will finally escort us Home."

Gram told us that her illness had given her more than it had taken away from her, and she truly believed that.

During Gram's hospital stays, I had time to talk with Mrs. Como as we drove back and forth to visit her. She was aware that I would not be returning to Hopewell after my Gram died. As I sat with her this morning, I could sense her sadness at the thought of my selling the farm and going back to New England.

"We would love to have you stay here with us, Tess. It's quiet here, and as you remember, things do not change very much," she said with a smile.

"I know that's true, Mrs. Como, and that is why Hopewell was such a great place to grow up," I said. "I thought long and hard about selling the farm. To tell you the truth, this morning outside the diner, I began to doubt my decision. However, I know I would miss my life and my work in Boston. I guess it is true, it is hard to come back, once you leave home."

She took my hand.

"Tess," she said, "your Gram worked very hard and saved diligently in order for you to go to fine schools, and get an excellent education. She watched you leave, and she missed you very much, but she was extremely proud of you when you graduated from the university. She had very high expectations for you. She would always tell us how good you were doing in your profession and show us pictures of all the interesting places in the world that you had been. She donated a copy of every book you wrote to the local library, so we could all get a chance to read it."

Her eyes filled with tears.

"You know, Tess, your Gram always said that someday she would bring you home again," Carmela said. "I do not know what she meant by that, but she sounded very sure that eventually you would come back."

"I know Mrs. Como, Gram did without a lot for herself in order for me to go away and study. She always encouraged me to make wise decisions, and she told me that it was as easy as connecting the dots between imagining something and making it happen." I continued. "Although she taught me that there is a reason for everything, I cannot believe that she wanted me to come back here and give up my prominent career and comfortable lifestyle. I just don't believe that fate is conspiring against me and luring me back to farm Gram's land. I'm sorry, Mrs. Como, I am determined not to let my heart rule my head.

Mrs. Como smiled calmly, and then spoke in a respectful tone of voice.

"Yes, your Gram always believed that everything happens for a reason however she also believed that we are given chances along the way to help guide us in the direction that is the best for us. They are the little lessons that are sent to us throughout our lives. If we can learn from them, our lives change for the better. Your Gram always tried to stay open to receiving them." She continued. "You know, Tess, all we can do is to keep our hearts open and just hope that we do not miss them."

With her eyes closed, she squeezed my hand.

"Yes, Tess, we must hope that we do not miss them."

The tea, cookies, and strawberries tasted so good. We talked and laughed for most of the afternoon, and there were many 'remember when,' and 'it seemed like just yesterday,' said. Jake sat patiently, and Mrs. Como rewarded him with litte effort. I felt so comfortable sitting here with her that I delayed my return to the farm. I simply lost track of time, and before I knew it, the evening was upon us. Mrs. Como looked tired and of course Jake, still at her feet, was fast asleep.

"I think we'll be heading back to the farm. What do you think, Jake?" I said.

He looked up at me and finally got to his feet.

"Come on, Jake, let's go."

Mrs. Como walked to the refrigerator and pulled out a bag.

"I packed some homemade food and goodies for you to enjoy, and I hope to see you again before you leave," she said.

"Mrs. Como, ever since I can remember, you have always been there for Gram and me. I know that you meant the world to her, and you mean the world to me too. If at any time you ever need anything, just let me know."

She nodded slowly. I kissed her gently on her cheek and gave her a hug. Then Jake and I headed for the car.

It was a beautiful night, and the full moon guided us back to the farm. Since Jake looked like he was anxious for some exercise, I headed out to the field with him. It was calm, but very cold. The moonlight created an incredible sight. The ice and snow storm from last night left its mark. The tall, bare trees looked as if they were soldiers surrounding the field, and when the moonlight reflected the ice on their branches, they looked as if they donned a coat of armor.

My down coat felt like a warm blanket, and my shoe grippers dug into the pristine ice. We walked carefully to the edge of the field, and I spotted the little chair that Gramps made for me.

I remember the day he gave it to me. He came into the house and told me to get on the tractor with him because he had a surprise to show me. He drove us out here.

"This is for you, Tess," he said.

As he helped me down from the high seat, I saw this little wooden chair with my name carved on the top sitting at the edge of the field. I remember being so thrilled with my surprise. I ran back and forth between Gramps and the chair, each time giving him a big hug. I could not believe that Gram kept it in the same place all these years.

Looking back toward the house, every window was illuminated by an electric candle. Gram insisted they stay lit continuously. She believed the candles were a sign that I was always welcome here, and that I would always find love and comfort within this house.

Even though it was cold out here, I wanted to sit on my chair for a while and think about my day. Ellie and Mrs. Como were part of a past that I had not taken the time to think about for a while. My visits here were always brief. I would drive down just to see Gram either for the weekend, or on my way to another job, and always with an urgency to get back on the road. The stars shone brightly in the night sky, and I realized it was an unusually long time since I gave them more than a passing glance. Jake was running all around the field, and as I was trying to keep him in sight, I caught a glimpse of a flickering light among the trees. At first, it looked like a candle flame being teased by the night breeze. It was coming from the woods on the other side of the house where the honeymoon hideout, and the Springhouse were located. I could not believe that Gram put an electric candle in any of those windows, since to my knowledge, there was no power going to those structures. Not knowing what to make of it, I immediately called to Jake, and we began to walk back toward the house. The light became brighter. Perhaps it was a nearby neighbor with a flashlight looking for something in the woods. Gram always let the neighbors on the land if the reason was valid, and everyone always respected her boundaries. We walked past the back entrance of the house and up to the edge of the woods until we reached the path that led to the Springhouse. Feeling no urgency to explore the dark forest, I went no further. Jake was not barking and seemed quite content and peaceful, so I considered the sighting as one of those unexplainable moments, and let it go with that. Heading back toward the house, I was startled for a moment by a silhouette standing behind the screen door. It looked just like my Gram. I stopped, and Jake's ears perked up.

"Do you see what I see, Jake?" I said.

After a few seconds of feeling overwhelmed, I calmly concluded that what I saw was a result of being tired from the events of the day and missing Gram so much. Still curious, I turned around to see if the flickering light was still visible, and, to my surprise, it had disappeared along with the shadow at the door. The wind began to whistle through the trees, and for a brief moment, I began to hear the same words in my mind that I heard the night before.

The world is full wonder, each time a new sun breaks
It leaves us with a story, as the moon and owl awake
The story is a message, for the open heart to take
The world is full wonder, each time a new sun breaks

Safely in the house, I bolted the door, lit the stove, and headed upstairs to bed.

Day Three

I awoke this morning with the sun streaming through the bedroom windows. When I motioned for Jake to follow me down the stairs, he jumped right up from his comfortable dog bed. He acquired the habit a few years ago of following Gram upstairs at night. Before that, he would curl up on the cozy couch downstairs to sleep. Gram felt that he needed a soft bed for his new sleeping arrangements, so she generously stuffed and stitched a wide sack together. She made it from some patchwork fabric that she had left over from another project.

"You spoil Jake," I would say to her.

"Doesn't matter now, does it Tess?" she would say, smiling at me. "I did a good job spoiling you too, and you turned out just fine."

Then she would give me a big hug. I missed that embrace this morning. I missed Gram this morning.

Jake knew it was time for breakfast, or from dog sense, at least time to beg for some food. The coffee tasted so good as I sipped it slowly at the kitchen table. It awakened me into the realization that one day went by, and I did nothing toward preparing the house for its planned sale. Today, I will head to the attic and start going through the boxes and trunks, I thought. By the end of today, I should have at least one room emptied and packed. Jake seemed ready to resume his nap on the couch, and comfortably positioned himself after he finished eating.

A door in Gram's room hid the steps to the attic. It was a simple construction providing a way to get from the second to the third floor. The stairway was original to the house, and it had seen the wear from many generations. The stairs remained unpainted just because they were not in a visible area. In the old days, families painted the parts of the house where people lived and company visited. With cardboard boxes in hand, I began my ascent. The stairs were a narrow passage to the attic, although the third level floor space spread out to cover the entire length and width of the house. The sun shown in the two small windows on the east side, and illuminated the pale green tasseled valences. Gray metal screens were in the bottom half of the windows to provide ventilation to the attic. The slight current of air coming through them moved the musty smell of the attic toward me, and with it, the nostalgic memories of my childhood. It was quiet up here today. The snow and ice lay heavy on the slate roof that slanted down on both sides of the attic. Even though it was slightly warmer today then yesterday, there was little hope that much of it would disappear. The third floor was cool, but not cold enough to stop me from carrying out my plans for the day.

As I looked around the attic, it was just as I remembered it when I was a child. This attic was every little girl's dream place, but I was the lucky one that got to call it her playhouse. I spent most of my weekends and other days off from school playing up here. It was just wonderful when it rained on those days, then I could hear the drops falling on the slate roof as I played. Closing my eyes, I remembered how cozy and comfortable that made me feel, and I realized that even now, I preferred an overcast day to a sunny one.
Gram helped me make a play kitchen from cardboard boxes, and we arranged them in the right-hand corner. To my amazement they were still there, dissembled and lying against the wall. My old doll crib, cradling about five of my childhood favorites, remained covered with a blanket. The table and chairs that Gramps made for me in his workshop were also covered. Through the plastic, I could see the miniature blue willow dishes and tea pot that I set for a tea party nearly fifty years ago. The two teddy bears and two baby dolls sat patiently on the chairs as if they were waiting for me to return before they began pouring the tea. I remember that I played up here for hours. Gram would have to call me two and three times to come for supper. I always came down very apologetic, and with the same excuse that I did not hear her.

Tea Party in the Attic

That was not exactly a lie. I remember being so absorbed in my make believe world that all else became irrelevant. Those were fantastic times as, once again, I realized that the years passed all too quickly.

I wanted to take with me the first doll that my mother and father gave to me, and a teddy bear that Gram and Gramps gave to me on my sixth birthday. That left two chairs empty at the tea table. I packed those treasures ever so gently in the box going to Boston. I decided to leave my make believe playhouse. Perhaps a family with small children would buy the farm, and another little girl would have the opportunity to turn this attic into her playroom. There were a few more boxes labeled 'Tess' that contained remembrances of special occasions. There was a high-school jacket, diploma, prom dress, and some cards and pictures from relatives, friends, and former classmates. I would also take them with me.

On the other side of the attic, there were two closets. One was Gram's own makeshift design that she used to keep her off season clothing, and the other one was a sturdy, wooden, walk-in closet that Gramps built. I loved to go into that closet because it always smelled from cedar, and Gram kept our warm coats, linens, and blankets in there. I always knew when she changed the summer bedspreads to winter quilts, because the cedar scent came with them. It was so comforting to settle into my bed and pull the blankets up around me. Even today, the smell of cedar brings to mind Grams commitment to keeping her family comfortable and warm.

An old, oak chest with a crocheted drape over it occupied the space between the two closets. In the center of the lace coverlet was a solid, oval piece of cloth, and the name, Anna Gia, was done in needlepoint. It was a while since I was in the attic, and I forgot that after my mother passed away, Gram and Gramps carried her hope chest up here from her room. Gram placed all of her remembrances in it. Preparing for the grief that always came over me when I thought about my mother, I unlocked the cedar chest and forced open the heavy cover. A narrow shelf jetted out from under the domed lid, and a small mirror lay behind the middle partition. I quickly moved away when I thought I saw the reflection of my mother's face in that mirror, but to my surprise, it was my own. I'm beginning to look just like my mother, I thought, and gave no further thought to the happening.

Anna Gia was born March 14, 1933, in the iron bed in Gram's bedroom. Doctor Hastings was there, but Gram always said that it was she, not he, that delivered mom.

"He helped a little, but I did all the hard work," she said. "It was a blessed time for me and your grandfather when your mother came to us. I remember as I was giving birth to her," she recalled with a tear in her eye, "Duke Ellington was singing, 'Sophisticated Lady' on the radio, and Gramps, knowing I loved that song, turned up the volume."

From what I could remember, my mother was a warm and gentle woman. She was about five foot one inch tall and had an average frame. She wore her dark hair at a medium length and styled it in a wave. Many people thought my mother to be pretty, but to me she was beautiful, loving, and strong. Gram said that she was a quiet little girl and, even when she grew up, she would listen more than she would speak. She knew many people and enjoyed being around them, but she treasured her personal time, either alone or with her two closest friends. She loved school and read a lot. Gram always thought that she would become a teacher, but she met my father when she was young, fell in love, and she got married. I think even though she loved working on the farm during the summers at Grams, during the school she lived through my father's academic career. When we lived in Abington, she volunteered in the school library, and I believe she did most of the research that he needed for his classes. For the most part, she taught me to read at an early age and encouraged me to read as many books as I possibly could. It was because of her that I learned to think beyond what I knew. Her influence remains with me today. At work, when I am forced to go over and above the obvious, I know she is right next to me. I realize that this gentle stirring within me is the presence of my mother's voice calling to me, to try harder, to do better, and raise the bar a little higher. These seemingly unexplainable moments of inspiration are the times when, even for a second, I am able to get past my own limited thinking, rise to the challenge, and I realize that anything less than excellence is a disservice to my public. When I look in the mirror, I am not surprised that I resemble my mother. I have the same expression and manner in my eyes as she had, and what an honor that is. Again, I thank God that I had her as my teacher, even if it was for a short time.

There were three framed pictures cuddled in my mother's lace wedding gown that Gram placed delicately inside the chest. The first picture was of my grandmother holding my mother at one year of age. The second was a picture of my mother. Anna Gia, age 17, was written on the back of the black and white photo. It was probably taken a year before she got married, I thought. The last picture was of my grandmother, my mother, and me. The photo was taken on the front porch of Gram's house, and we all looked so very happy. My grandmother's arm was around my mother's shoulder, and my mother held my Gram's hand. A young version of me, balanced on one foot and squinting at the camera, stood in front of them. The fact that mom and Gram were always so accepting of the imperfect was evident from the looks of me. I treasured these pictures. Looking at their images, I felt so grateful for all that they had done for me. These two remarkable women had been part of my journey. It has been an incredible ride, I thought. At that moment, I felt humbled, a feeling I had not experienced in a very long time.

Under the wedding gown and veil, there was a book titled 'Heidi' by Johanna Spyri. It was my mother's favorite book. The cover was faded, and the pages were yellowed. These were the indelible marks of time and use. This copy was published in 1915, and belonged to my great-grandmother. 'Happy Birthday, Anna Gia, from Grandma Mary,' was inscribed on the first page. Gram said that her mother gave the book to my mother on her ninth birthday. After she read it, she would not let it out of her sight.

I did not remember too much about my mother because I was only ten years old when she died. While she was sick, my Gram became her caregiver, and when the disease became irreversible, Gram guided her toward the Spirit that they both ardently believed in and loved. I remember I would sit on the bed while she held my mother's hand. The doctor would put cool cloths on her head and provide the best medicine he had. Gram would talk to her of a Place that was so beautiful and filled with infinite love and light and peace. She reassured her that when the time came, she would be with her, and hold unto her hand in this world, until her God embraced her in the next.

Gram taught us to be loving and forgiving even when it was difficult to love and forgive.

"Do it anyway," she would say. She taught us from her heart, not a book, with extraordinary humility and respect.

"Be patient when you don't have the all the answers. Give it to that infinite universal power, and you will be surprised what comes back to you."

She always saw the best in other people and had no patience for doom and gloom. She found her joy in living, and had a passion for life. She invented herself from the soul outward. She looked at her life as a journey, using the finite world and her role in it, to grow and learn, as she made her way back to her Higher Presence.

My mother started the final of part her journey Home in early March, and she reached her Destination on March 22, 1963. Gram and Gramps tried to comfort me the best way that they knew.

"You know Tess, your mother is not sick anymore. Her spirit is in Heaven, and wherever love exists. In your heart, she is alive and happy," Gram would tell me. "Your mother entrusted us with someone very precious, and we will take very good care of you."

Gram was right. She and Gramps took wonderful care of me, and I could not have asked for a better family. When I'd feel lonesome for my mother, my Gram would take me for a walk around the Springhouse, tell me to be very quiet, and listen for my mother's voice. After standing there with my eyes closed for a few seconds, I would open them, giggle, and tell her that I did not hear anything.

"It's all in how you listen, Tess," she would say. "It's all in how you listen."

Then we would go into the house, and bake chocolate chip cookies. Gramps would tell me that these special cookies were in honor of my mom because the Chocolate Chip Cookie was invented in 1933, the year my mother was born. Gramps always loved to read the history of just about anything, and was always filling us in on what he knew. Gram and I would laugh because after he told us about the Chocolate Chip Cookie invention, he would go through the other trivia of 1933. He continued.

"Did we know that the cost of a new house was $5,750.00; the average earnings per year were $1500.00; Gas cost 12 cents a gallon; a loaf of bread, 7 cents; a pound of hamburger meat, 11 cents, and a new car around $600.00. Now in 1913, when your Gram was born, a new home costs $3,395.00; the average amount of money people earned was $1,296.00; Gas costs 10 cents a gallon; and a loaf of bread was 6 cents; a gallon of milk, 36 cents, and a new car, $490.00. Yep, and that's the truth," he said, puffing on his pipe filled with Prince Albert tobacco.

Gram and I would laugh and roll our eyes, and before I knew it, the sadness of missing my mom was gone. I continued to grow up in this nurturing home, with all its warmth and comfort. Amazingly, I felt it at this moment.

On the floor of the chest, I found my mother's white beaded wedding album, her wedding jewelry, a gold necklace and matching bracelet, wrapped in a white silk pouch. A little blue cardboard, 'Just Married' sign was next to it. I took some time to go through some other photo collections of my father, and some pictures of all of us together that were saved in a shoe box in the chest. A few fashionable hats and stylish dresses that my mother wore, and a lavender afghan Gram knitted to keep my mother warm when she became ill, were folded and placed under the photos. I knew that many of these things would live beyond me. They already lived a life of their own. Now they were becoming entwined with my story and moving on through me. These possessions all bore a trace of my family, who I loved and missed so much. I made a mental note that I would be taking the cedar chest with me. I closed it and replaced the drape.

I could see the sun setting through the west side windows. I cannot believe that I've been up here all day, I thought. I looked around the attic, and saw very little packed and ready to go.

Jake was still lying on his couch when I walked downstairs. He jumped up and readied himself by the door when he saw me.

"Too late to prepare supper, Jake," I said, so we headed out to the diner. I had meatloaf and mashed potatoes, dining at the table, and Jake had the same, only his was take out. I started the car and waited a few moments to turn on the heater. In the meantime, Jake was finishing up his supper in the back seat and, by the sound of it, trying to retrieve the last morsel from the plastic container.

"You know Jake," I said, "I did not get too much done today, but for some reason, I feel as if I had a particularly memorable day. I found myself somewhere that I did not expect to be, and I found myself reminiscing some childhood memories."

Stretched out on the back seat of the car, Jake did not seem to have an opinion one way or the other. With a full belly, he settled in for a comfortable ride home.

The air smelled so fresh and crisp tonight, and the sky was clear with the stars and moon preparing for a spectacular display of their elegant beauty. If I took the main road back to the farm, I would be there in fifteen minutes, so I decided to enjoy the night and take the longer way back to Gram's house. The night is clear, and the moon is full, I thought, and I was in no hurry. Somewhere in my mind, I knew the road I decided to take twisted around the bend that encircled the church and cemetery where my mother and father, my Gram and Gramps, and the rest of my family were buried. Even though it was dark, I felt an unexplainable urge to visit their graves. I turned left at the church and parked in front of the black, rod iron, cemetery gate.

Opening the glove compartment, I retrieved my flashlight that I kept stowed away for emergencies, stepped out of the car, and opened the back door for Jake to jump out. I pulled the gate toward me. It squeaked. The moon light revealed the gravestones in front of me, and the circle of artificial light illuminated my path.

"I wonder if people that know that they are going to die believe that nothing they do that day is worth any of their time, Jake." I said softly. "Perhaps, we human beings think too much of ourselves. Why the time for all of us together on this earth is a split second, and for just one of us, it is so brief that we cannot even begin to give it a name."

We made our way down the path to the pile of loose soil where my Gram's ashes were buried a few days ago. I stood there in disbelief, but the wilted flowers, still lying on the ground, confirmed the truth. Next to Gram and my Gramps grave was my mother's and my father's resting place. It was marked by a gray concrete slab that rose about a foot from the ground. Their names appeared separately on each side with the dates of their birth and death chiseled into the rock.

Entrance to the Cemetery

Jake laid down and positioned himself politely on the side of the grave.

Oh! How I wish I could at least have one more day with them, I thought. I know that for the entire day, I would hold them close, tell them I love them, and thank them for the sacrifices they made for me. Kneeling down on the cold ground, I shifted the light toward my mother's side of the grave. A small, golden, glass cup was fixed in a copper holder and sat beneath my mother's name. I remember Gram believed that the gold light signified a higher power, infinite wisdom, and love. She faithfully kept a candle burning in that glass for her beloved daughter. I made a mental note to bring it with me, since Gram would no longer be around to revive the flame. I tilted the flashlight until I was focused on her name.

"My mother, my nurse, my teacher, my friend," I whispered. "Today I was reminded of all the things we shared like your sweetness and your generosity, your warmth and caring. You were a truly remarkable woman, and I was so lucky to have been given such a gift. Please mother, help me find some meaning in my life. For the first time, I feel lost and unsure. I closed my eyes as if I had just finished a heartfelt prayer.

Then I will never forget what happened next.

The air seemed to blow colder, and Jake began to whimper. The flashlight began to fail. It flickered off and on, and finally went out. Jake was up on all fours and ready to go. I took hold of his collar and, as I did, I could feel the hair on the back of his neck beginning to stand up.

"Easy Jake," I said. "We're going."
Bending over to pick up the gold glass cup, I immediately pulled away my hand when I unexpectedly saw a little flame emerging. It looked as if someone had just lit a new candle, and the fire was making its way down the wick to the wax cake.

"Wait Jake," I said.

The Graves

Scared but unwilling to leave, I knelt down again in front of the grave. The flame gained more power, and was magnified shining through the golden glass. It was illuminating some words that were imprinted at the base of the gravestone. Words that I never noticed were there before. I moved closer, and as the candle blazed, I began to read,

The world is full wonder, each time a new sun breaks
It leaves us with a story, as the moon and owl awake
The story is a message, for the open heart to take
The world is full wonder, each time a new sun breaks

In utter amazement, I read the words again, until I couldn't see them any longer. The candle was going out, and the glass soon returned to its dormant state. I drove home silently.

Day Four

Jake and I slept until 10 o'clock the next morning, and I woke up wondering exactly what happened last night. I remembered that Gram once told me that the spirits have power.

"Many a religion give testament to it," she would say however I chose to believe differently. For some reason, returning to Hopewell for Gram's funeral was different than my other visits. I felt that living in this house without her, even for a few days, persuaded my thoughts and feelings to run riot. I began to see and hear things that were not there. Perhaps what I experienced last night, or what I thought I experienced last night, just showed the emotional stress that Gram's illness and death was having on me. I found myself drifting in and out of that confined space where longing meets reality. I just wanted to get past all this, return home and go on living as before.

Today was another day, and I decided to pack up Gram's room and get moving on the sale of the house and farm. I took the boxes upstairs after breakfast, and like the attic, I would pack the things that were going with me to Boston and leave the rest for a yard sale or auction.

Gram's room always smelled like perfume. On festive occasions, she would wear the special Chantilly fragrance that Gramps bought for her on her birthdays. Gram was a lovely lady. She was about five feet two inches tall and thin. She always wore her hair pinned up in a bun, with a fancy clip to secure it. When I was a little girl, I would go into her room and look at her round, face powder box and her slender, perfume atomizer sitting on an oval mirror on her dresser. This dark stained dressing table stood between two large windows. Gram placed it there so she could have the best lighting when she dressed and put on her makeup, or as she would say 'put on her face.'

Gram's Dresser

Two beautiful, Victorian lamps were on each side of the dresser, and she lit them while brushing her long hair at night. After Gram finished, she would pull all the hair out of the brush, and, rolling it into a ball, she would insert it into the hole in the lid of a round glass jar. Every chance I had to sneak into her room, I did, and I would stand in front of the dresser's long beveled mirror. I would pretend to spray on her perfume, and then dab my face with the puff that she kept inside of the powder box. Those sweet days from the past, I thought, when the most critical decision of the day was which one of Gram's dresses I would try on, and who I would pretend to be when I wore it.

Today, my intentions were decidedly different. I sat on the bench in front of the mirror and began to go through the dresser drawers. The first small drawer had all her nicely pressed handkerchiefs in it. Some had colorful crocheted edges, and others were just plain. There was one that Mrs. Como made for her. It was ivory with her name stitched in gold. That one was in a plastic bag, and it looked like it was never used. Knowing Gram, I believed that to be true. On top of the handkerchief was a black book labeled, 'My Poems.' From time to time, I remember I would see Gram writing in this book. When I asked her what she was doing, she would tell me that she was writing down some ideas that came into her mind.

"Someday, I may even write a book, Tess," she would say.

A small sachet of what looked and smelled like rose hips was next to the book and handkerchiefs. The middle drawer had her silks in it. There were three dressing gowns, some silk slips and panties, a pair of stockings, and another sachet of rose hips for fragrance. I placed them in the bag, along with the handkerchiefs to take to Mrs. Como, in case she wanted to use them. She would be thrilled to see the way Gram cared for the gift that she gave to her. The bottom drawer was next and it was the largest in the set of three. I smiled when I saw the contents. It had all the letters, greeting cards, and postcards that I sent to her from Boston, and different parts of the world. Under the cards, and lying on the bottom of the drawer, were the signed copies of the three books that I wrote. I had the publisher customize them for her, so I could give them to her on her seventy-fifth birthday. The contents of this drawer went into a box for Boston. The three drawers on the left-hand side of the dresser resembled the right. The first small one contained Gram's hair nets and fancy hair pins, along with some Bobbie pins, rollers, and perm rods. The last two larger drawers had Gram's hats, a small box of hat pins, and a few pieces of jewelry, all of which I wanted to keep. The long, middle drawer, which separated the right side of the dresser from the left had a decorative brass keyhole, and a key resting in it. Turning it clockwise, I heard a click, and the drawer opened easily as I pulled it toward me. The drawer contained a rectangular steel box, about three inches deep. It had a lock on it, and the key was taped to the lid. Gram's spiritual books were on the other side of the drawer. I removed the box and set it on my lap.

I vaguely remember the time when Gram asked Gramps to make this box for her, giving him the exact dimensions that she wanted him to use.

"Be sure it is steel and well built," she said to him, "and please place a small lock on the latch when you finish. I have important things to place in that box, Gramps."
She smiled and gave him a kiss on the cheek. Now I was about to see the importance of what she put inside. I heard Jake coming up the steps from the kitchen. He sat down along side of me and slowly reclined to my feet. It seemed like he was also waiting to see what was in the box.

"I bet you already know what Gram stashed in here, Jake. You don't fool me. You knew everything that went on around here."
The key snapped open the lock, and the lid flung open. Gramps put spring hinges on it, and I smiled thinking that he made it extra special for Gram because she gave him a big kiss. A blue envelope, labeled Last Will and Testament, was

the last thing Gram put in the box, and the first thing I saw. Underneath it, there was another sealed envelope with my name on it. It contained two keys, and a short message from Gram with some directions.

Dear Tess,
Upon my death, I am requesting that you take this note and the two keys in the envelope to our local bank in Hopewell. Ask for Janice, you remember her, and she will help you obtain what I have prepared for you.
Love Always and Forever,
Gram

Brushing my hand over her name, tears came to my eyes. I looked down at Jake and then up into the mirror. After taking a minute to decide what I was going to do, I picked up the Will, the note, and the keys, and headed to my car.

It was one-thirty when I arrived at the bank. I parked the car in the lot and walked across the street. The building looked the same as it did when Gram and I use to come here. I entered the gray cement building through the thick glass double doors.

The first person I saw was Eunice. She was busy at work behind the tall, marble counter that separated her from the customer's waiting line. Eunice was the bank's manager, and she was exceedingly proficient at what she did. She had a habit of looking toward the door as customers entered. If Eunice knew the person, she would nod and give them a welcoming smile. If she did not know the individual, she would still acknowledge them, but her expression was more reserved and guarded. As long as I could remember, the Hopewell bank had a sterling reputation. It was no secret that it gained that distinction because of Eunice's expertise and professionalism in leading the staff. As usual, she looked very professional. Eunice always dressed in a two piece suit with a flawlessly pressed blouse. She wore her long, light brown hair pinned up behind her head. As I entered the bank, she looked over her black framed glasses, and greeted me with a smile. She then continued with her work.

There were no customers around which was not unusual for a small bank mid day. It was so quiet and dignified, almost like a church after the service was over. I took a seat outside of the office door that had Janice's name on it and waited for her.

Janice had been with the Hopewell Bank a long time, starting here when she was about twenty-one. She was about five feet four inches tall, average build, blond hair, and was always well dressed for her position. She was the bank's customer service director, and she earned every bit of the respect that people gave her. She was attentive, friendly, and knew all of her customers by their first and last name. She took a genuine interest in who you were, and what you did. The community loved her. Throughout the years, as I was growing up, I always admired her.

When I was about eleven or twelve, Gram brought me to the bank to open a Christmas club, and I remember we waited outside of her office for fifteen minutes until Janice was available to help us. Gram would not do business with anyone else but Janice. After I was grew up, I thought about her especially around Christmas time. I think it was because of what she told me that day.

"Do you know, Tess, what makes a Christmas club so special? Every time you put money into it, you can think about the person that you will buy a gift for and wish them well."

She walked out of her office to see if anyone was waiting for her when she finished with her phone conversation.

"Hello Tess," she said, as if she expected to see me there. She reached out to hug me.

"I was waiting for you to arrive." She embraced me again, and kissed me on the cheek.

She was just as warm and loving as I remembered, although she looked some years older. Her hair was gray now, and some wrinkles formed around her eyes and her mouth. Gram told me that her husband, Richard, died a few years ago. I wanted to remember to offer my condolences, and ask about her children and her grandchildren. Taking my hand, Janice escorted me into her office and motioned for me to sit down on her beautifully flowered, upholstered chair. She circled around her desk and took her seat behind it.

"My, Tess, it is so good to see you, she said. When I saw you at your Gram's service, I could not believe that you are probably somewhere in your fifties already. You know, I am very close to seventy. My, life comes at us fast, doesn't it? I remember when they hired me here, and now I am getting ready to retire," she said, waving her hand across all the paperwork on her desk. "Why, it seems like just yesterday when you and your grandmother made visits to the bank. It sure has been an adventure, and from what your Gram has told me, it sounds as if yours has been a very exciting and rewarding one as well. Just think, Tess, a walk then a run on a path that leads us back to where we started. I guess all things are possible. Have you decided when you will be moving back to the farm?"

"I'm not coming back to the farm, Janice," I said looking down at the floor. "I have decided to put Gram's house and farm on the market, go back to Boston, and take up my life where I left off."

"Oh, I'm sorry, Tess, I was under the impression from talking to your Gram that you would be taking over the farm when she passed on," she said.

"Don't get me wrong, Janice, but the truth is that I could never be satisfied just living on the farm. I need to be surrounded by my challenging work, and very interesting people."

I hesitated when I heard myself say that. Janice just smiled.

"Well, I wish you the best with your decision," she said. She looked down at her desk for a moment, and then back toward me. She continued.

"Funny thing about our choices, Tess, at times they can fool us into believing we are different than we really are."

She stood up behind her desk.

"If I hear of someone that may want to buy the property, I will contact you. I know you would like to see it in good hands. We all would. Your Gram loved that farm. It was her haven. Now, what can I help you with today, dear?" she asked.

I pulled the blue envelope that contained Gram's Last Will and Testament out of my purse, along with the envelope that contained the note and the keys.

"I found this is Gram's steel box as I was cleaning out her dresser," I said, handing her the envelope. "The note says that I should come to the bank and ask for you, and you will help me with it. So here I am. I was aware of her Will, Janice, but I'm not sure about anything else."

Janice reached across the desk, opened the envelop, and quickly read the note.

"Oh, yes," she said. "Your Gram, our lawyer, and I discussed this matter some time ago when she was trying to get her final papers together. She was very particular that all was in order, and that you were named, as you know, her sole heir."

Tears came to my eyes. She continued.

"The keys belong to our customer's safe deposit boxes, and your Gram used the system to store important papers and things that she wanted you to have," she said. "According to her Will, I have permission to release the contents to you now. The bank keeps special carriers for our customers, so you will have a safe method of transporting the contents. It all belongs to you. Please follow me."

I got up from my chair and followed Janice out of her office. We walked to back of the bank and entered a gate that lead to a large steel vault. She moved some dials, pulled open the door, and we walked into the secured area. Silver drawers of all sizes lined the side walls. A smaller steel vault lined the back wall. She motioned for me to step over to the desk, opened the drawer, and pulled out a black book. After signing my name beneath the date and correct time that she recorded, she led me to the box labeled 333. Taking my key and adding one of her own, she pulled out the drawer. I followed her to a small booth next to the vault. She told me to take my time, and that she would return shortly with the carrier.

The original Last Will and Testament lay right on top. Under that were Gram's birth certificate, Gramps death certificate, Jake's ownership papers, my college diploma, and my first Christmas club book from the bank. There were other pertinent documents concerning the farm, such as the deed, and the satisfied mortgage record that showed no lien or judgment against the property. There were other documents that validated my ownership of the farm. In a black velvet pouch, Gram saved Gramps old Hamilton watch, mom's platinum wedding and engagement rings, her gold wedding band and a matching diamond ring, and a pearl ring. When I saw the pearl ring, I took a deep breath. Gram had given me that ring when I graduated from high school. I put it on. It used to fit my ring finger, I thought, but now only fit my little finger.

I remembered the time she had given that ring to me. It was for my high school graduation. She was so proud of herself for choosing a perfect gift for me. Today, I was heartbroken thinking about my carelessness in leaving this ring behind when I moved to Boston. She must have been disappointed when she found it in my room. She saved it all these years for me. I hoped that Gram understood the unwise decisions of being young. That thought helped a little with my regret.

"Thank you, Gram," I whispered, as I secured the ring on my finger.

When Janice returned, we both felt the sadness moving between us as she helped me put everything in the carrier. I gave Janice a hug and thanked her for all that she did for Gram and me.

As I was about to leave the secure area, Janice reached for my arm as if to stop me.

"Tess," she said, "did you forget about the other box?"

I turned to her with an unusually puzzled look on my face.

"Tess, the envelope contained two keys."

58

"I know, Janice," I said, "but the bank usually gives two keys for a safe deposit box, don't they?"

"Yes, today they do, but when your Gram rented the boxes, things were different. At that time, our bank issued only one key per box. There is another box here that belongs to you."

She led me over to the section that stored the larger boxes, and as her eyes ran down the row of numbers, her hand reached out for box 802. Again, using both keys, she unlocked the door, and pulled out the box.

"Tess," she said, "may I stand here with you while you open it?"

"Sure, Janice, I have no idea what Gram would have put in another box. Do you know?"

Smiling, she motioned for me to open the box. Lifting the tin cover, I could see an item enclosed in white tissue paper. When I removed the covering, I could hardly believe my eyes. There she was, my old doll Annie. I looked at Janice and then back at the doll.

"Gram and I made her together," I said. "Gram had boiled some tea and soaked a piece of her white cotton cloth in it so that we could make Annie out of a tea stained fabric. We called her, 'Poka Dot Annie,' because we made her a dress from some red polka dot material, and we sewed on red buttons that Gram had in her button jar."

Annie had a wide body and long, spindly, arms and legs. She measured about 24 inches long, when we finished stuffing her with cotton. I cut the dark red yarn for her hair, and Gram pasted it across the top her head and formed it into two short pony tails on each side. I was glad to have the doll again, but I did not understand why Gram put her in a safe deposit box.

"Janice, do you know why she did this?" I asked.

Again, she smiled.

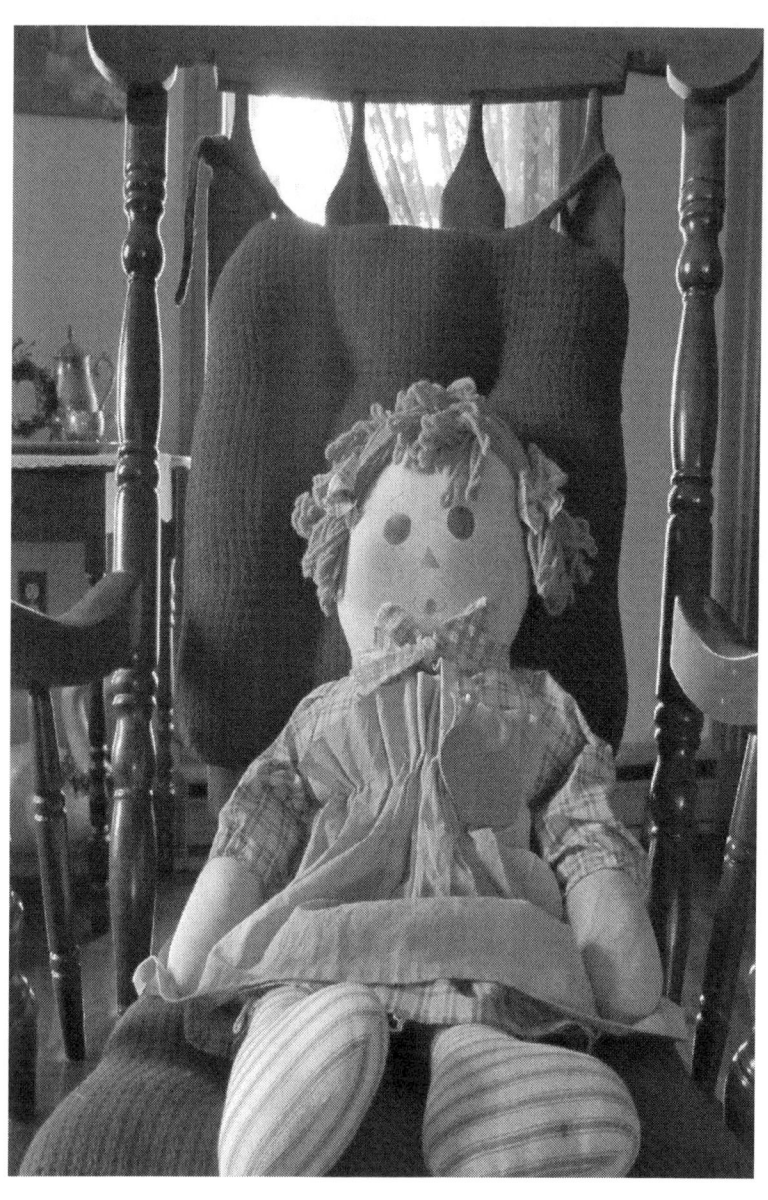

Annie

"Just let me say that your Gram thought of everything." Still not understanding any of it, I wrapped the doll in the tissue paper and said good-bye to Janice. I placed my treasure in the carrier and walked out to my car.

It was getting dark as I drove back to the farm. Jake and I shared some dinner and we went for a walk. When we got back into the house, Jake jumped on the couch, and I settled into the rocking chair next to a cozy fire with my old friend, Annie.

When I was eleven years old, Gram and I made her on a rainy Sunday afternoon. Gram was sewing a dress for herself, and I begged her to let me sew something too. She put away her project, and together we sat down and made the doll. It took us all afternoon. I remember we had such a good time, but I also remember that we disagreed about something. What was it now? I thought for a while. I believe she wanted to add something to the doll that I did not want. What was it? I thought. Then I remembered. Gram wanted to make an opening in the back of Annie's body, so that I would have a safe place to hide things.

"Everyone needs a secret hiding place that only they know about," she said. "This could be yours."
Gram got her way, and she began to cut and stitch. When she finished, she fastened the gap with four eye hooks so that I could easily open it.

Turning over the doll that laid on my lap, I unbuttoned the dress and, sure enough, there was the opening. Releasing each hook carefully, I could not believe what I found inside. She stuffed money, in all forms, into the doll. Money, I believe, that came from her inheritance, and some that she saved on her own. There were tightly wound rolls of fifty and hundred dollar bills. There were several CD's in varying amounts in my name. Bonds and annuities that she had set aside for me, and a trust fund document, were carefully packed into this doll. I could not believe my eyes. A folded piece of paper was safety pinned near the doll's chest, right around where Annie's heart would be found. It was in

Gram's handwriting. I unpinned the note, slowly unfolded it, and began to read.

Tess,

Life is full of lovely things to enjoy. There are magnificent sunrises and soft sunsets. There are walks in the park where love and laughter can be heard. There are quiet moments to enjoy, fragrant blossoms to smell, and falling snowflakes to walk through. Yes, Tess, we all need some money, but all the money in the world cannot reproduce a sunset on the ocean, or give you a cool breeze on a hot August day. Search for the music that makes your heart and your soul want to dance. Follow the music out to dance floor, Tess. Embrace it and move with it, for the world is full of wonder, each time a new sun breaks, and it leaves us with a story as the moon and owl awake. The story is a message for the open heart to take. The world is full of wonder, each time a new sun breaks.

Love to you always and forever..

Gram

Oh...and don't forget to plant rosemary by your front door.

Tears streamed down my face. I clutched the note and doll to my chest as if I was embracing my new born baby.
What was Gram trying to tell me? I thought.
Then as if I were answering her from across the room, I said out loud,
"Yes, Gram, I live my life at a crazy pace, but I have to live that way to stay on top. I do not want to give up the awards or the rewards. Not yet Gram. No, not yet."

Day Five

When Gram was still alive, and her workdays on the farm became repetitive or tiring, she would give Gramps a hint that she wanted to get away for the day. I remember Gramps would be just too pleased to oblige. He would load me, and Gram, and his fishing gear into the car, and off we would go to Herron. Gram loved that place and called it the most peaceful spot on Earth. It was well known by many of the people in Hopewell, especially the fishermen, who headed there for a day or weekend of fine angling, and the fishing news.

Driving to Herron was my plan for this unseasonably warm late March day. Since the snow and ice from the storm at the beginning of the week began to melt this morning, it started to feel more like spring.

A quick stop at the bank to deposit the money and to thank Janice for her help was first on the list. She was with a customer when I came through the door. As she looked up, and our eyes met, the calm nod of her head, and the smile on her face, confirmed her delight in being able to carry out Gram's last wishes.

With diner coffee in hand, and some music on the radio, Jake and I headed north, then west, then north again. I barely remembered the directions, but Jake did not seem to mind as he rode shotgun with his head out the window. After driving about three hours, we managed to arrive at the road that led to the canyon. Bearing left, we followed the road for six more miles, and pulled into the parking lot.

I cannot say what triggered the getaway from the farm today. Perhaps it was my early rising. Perhaps it was the temptation to spend some time outdoors, I just did not know. However, I awoke with this strange, nagging urge to head toward Herron.

When I was in my early twenties, Gram and I would come here to talk and spend the day while walking the trails in the canyon. She had one trail that she loved more than any other. "I call this one, 'Heaven's Gate,' Tess." She continued. "When I leave this earth and head back from where I came, I believe I will walk down a path that looks just like this one. As I walk, my life will be reviewed. The farther I go, the clearer my vision will become. I will begin to see, through the eyes of my Spirit and other great teachers, the good that I have done, as well as the hurt and pain that I have caused others. I will begin to see my place and connection in the grand scheme of things, and the Divine Plan.

I believe, Tess, that the spirit repeatedly takes on a human body to evolve, finding itself back at a human birth many times, seeking real change for itself. It's like the spirit takes a short nap and comes back to pick up where it has left off. Sometimes it may even migrate toward people in its past lives. For instance, a chance meeting of someone that looks familiar, but you cannot recall, yet you immediately like. A dejavu, if you will. The human mind cannot remember, but the spirit never forgets."

Maybe Gram's words brought me here today, I thought. Looking around, I wanted to experience the peace I use to feel when I came here, but for some reason, it escaped me today. The imbalance felt disturbing.

From the top of the canyon, the view was so incredible, that I realized why Gram used the word, magnificent to describe it. Jake and I stood at a vista on the west side of the canyon. Millions of years ago, before time had a name, swift-moving waters carved out this canyon and moved the earth to pose these mountains, I thought. Now I stand here today, looking at the design of that ancient Intellect. As far as the eye could see, there were trees with bare branches that were just beginning to reveal their green buds. Tall evergreens took their stance among them and, all in their own right, seemed to be following a Divine Plan.

I suddenly felt so small standing beside this vast wonder.

Herron's West Rim

For a split second, it occurred to me that out of the thousands of acres out here, there was not one of them that cared about my fame, my money, the books I published, or the awards I carried home. All this that surrounded me was greater than anything I could ever be, or could ever imagine being, yet I contained every part of its majestic whole. For the first time in a long time, I was experiencing life in its purest form. Jake sat silently watching a hawk circle. It almost looked as if he were contemplating his connection and place in this great family tree.

The temperature today was an indication that spring was on its way. Gated at the edge, I could still lean far enough over to see the large creek waters streaming along on the floor of the canyon. It was early for fishing, but the tiny specks I saw along the water were the die-hard fisherman of the season.

My Gramps was an incredible fly fisherman. He tied his own flies, studied the water and, although he listened to the advice of the experts, he learned the best from observing the streams around him. His father, Pasquale, taught him and his younger brother, Frank, fly fishing when they were young. His father had a passion for the art, and wanted to pass that on to his sons. That is exactly what he did.

"We would come to these streams every chance we had," he would tell me. "My father, my brother, and I would fish from morning until night, camp out, and get up the next morning and start again. When my father got too old, and his arthritis got the best of him, we built him a chair. My brother and I would help him walk, one of us on either side of him, from the trail to the edge of the stream. Then he would sit down on the chair, and my brother and I would carry the chair and him into the middle of stream so he could fish. He never caught too many fish that way, but he never gave up trying. Yes, Tess, his passion lived on through us."
Just like his father, my Gramps could never get enough of fishing these streams.

Herron Creek Canyon

Although he came here with his friends, he was glad when Gram had enough with the work and wanted to head for Herron. One day, Gramps told me a secret and made me promise never to tell Gram. He said that sometimes he would constantly ask her to help him with chores and repairs, just to get her to that point.

"It's funny your Gram never figured out that I would ask her to help me with more projects during the best fishing months," he said with a sly grin on his face, as we sat on the porch rockers, and he smoked his pipe. Gramps never realized that Gram was standing at the screen door listening to him, and lovingly shaking her head.

"Come on Jake, don't you think it's time for a hike?" I said. "Walking outdoors will be beneficial for both of us." I knew as Gram grew older, Jake's walks became less frequent, and when she got really sick, they became non-existent. Since I had been at Gram's, I was starting to realize how much I actually missed being outdoors. At home, in Boston, my walk took place on a rubber mat attached to a machine that would go as fast and as steep as I programmed it to go. For a brief moment, the thought of going back to that, after having all of this, did not seem that attractive. I definitely did not want to stay in Hopewell, but all of a sudden, I wanted things to be back like they were.

The moment and thought passed when we reached the marker that said, 'Goat Path.' It was a mile long dirt path that led to the bottom of the canyon. Signs along the way warned hikers of steep and hazardous sections. There were areas that were beginning to erode from the natural spring waters flowing over them, so I put Jake on the leash and down we went. As we walked, we could see the sun shining through the tall pines that surrounded us. There were waterfalls, just like I remembered. Gram was right. It was the most peaceful setting on this earth. It took us about an hour to reach the bottom, where the path opened unto an old railroad bed that was turned into a bike path. Removing his lead, Jake tore across the path and headed down a small hill that led straight to the water. By the time I reached him, Jake was swimming in circles and lapping up what had to be unusually cold water. We walked along the edge of Herron Creek for a while, and when we did not see any fishermen around, I threw a stick into the water for Jake to retrieve.

"We would not want to scare the fish away, would we, Jake?" I said sarcastically. "I don't think that the fish are swimming in this cold water today anyway."

Gramps would tell me that fly fishermen did not necessarily go to the waters just to catch fish. Any day would bring out men and women that loved nature and had a passion for the stream. We saw some today fulfilling that prophecy.

We rounded the bend and saw an old iron foot bridge that crossed over the creek. A beautiful red-tailed hawk perched itself on the hand railing and did not seem startled by our presence.

"I do not know why, but Gram's favorite bird was the hawk," I said, talking out loud to Jake. "She said that it seemed as if it had command of the sky as it glided through the air. She always considered it an honor when she saw one circle the fields of her farm."

Jake paid no attention to me. As we walked closer to the bridge though, the hawk seemed to stare at us. Then with a graceful uplift, stretched its wings and took off down through the canyon.

Jake had the time of his life today, but the afternoon was waning, and we had to re-climb the Goat Path and drive back to Grams. Just as we were crossing over the bike trail, Jake's ears and tail perked up as he heard his name being called.

"Jake, Jake," the deep voice called. "Hi boy. It's me." Looking to his right, the dog hesitated, and then ran toward a tall figure walking toward us. From what I could see, he was wearing bulky waders, a wide brimmed hat, and carrying a fly rod. The man knelt down on one knee as Jake came up to him. He lowered his head so that Jake could lick his face, an action that dogs invented to express their fondness for someone they love.

Canyon Bridge

Since I did not recognize the person, I stayed back and waited. After they exchanged greetings, Jake started walking toward me, hesitated, then turned around and walked the other way. The dog was asking his friend to follow him. Obliging Jake, the figure moved closer.

"Hello," he said, "I'm Jake's veterinarian, Luke LeFevre. I hope I didn't startle you, but I thought I recognized Jake, one of my favorite patients.

He moved closer, so we could shake hands.

"Hi, I'm Tess." My grandmother was Angeline, Jake's owner," I said.

"Was?" he said, "I knew she was very sick, but I did not hear that she may have passed. Is she no longer with us?" He looked sad.

"Gram died about a week ago, and we are both trying to get through it the best way we can," I said, gently petting Jake on the head.

"I'm so sorry for you and your family. Your grandmother was a very special lady."

"Thank you, Luke," I said, "but I'm all that is left of her family. I'm here to take care of Jake and carry out Gram's last wishes."

Luke looked as if he were in his late fifties. He was about five feet ten or eleven inches tall, average build, and from what I could see from under the brim of his hat, pleasant looking.

"Now I remember," he said, "your Gram mentioned you in many of our conversations. You live in Boston, right?"

"Yes, that's right, and I will be going back there soon," I replied in somewhat of a defensive tone.

"So you will not be moving back and taking over the farm?" Luke asked. "I always thought that Angeline wanted the farm to stay in the family, and hearing you say that you were the only one left, I'm sorry, but I assumed that you were going to be the one to keep it."

"No, my home and my work are in Boston," I said abruptly.

71

Luke LeFevre

"How about Jake, will he be going with you?" Luke asked.

"Yes, of course. He is a great dog and was Gram's best friend. I will give him a very good home. He knows me and likes me well enough," I said, nervously patting Jake on his head.

"It sure looks that way. If you want, bring him by the clinic for a quick check up before you leave, just to make sure he is in the best of health. Here is my card."
He reached into his green shirt pocket and pulled out a white card dotted with black paw prints.

"The clinic name, address, and phone number are on there. I'll give my friend a once over. It will be a goodbye present from me."

The card simply read,
The Animal Clinic
Luke LeFevre, Veterinary Doctor
Phone – 484-553-4011

"Thanks," I said, "I'll do that."
Trying to change the subject about not keeping the farm, I quickly asked,
"How is the fishing today?"

"Not so good," he said, shaking his head.

"They are just waking up from a long winter's nap. I thought I might find a couple that were really hungry, or maybe just a little newsy. Today isn't my usual day out of the office. The other Vet that works for me called and said that something unexpectedly came up with his family this morning, and would I mind switching our days off. I didn't really mind, but since I had no plans for the day, the idea to drive up to Herron suddenly popped into my mind. Well, I never have to think twice about coming to Herron and doing some fishing. Besides, it's a beautiful day for a drive.

"Do you fish, Tess?" Luke asked.

"No, no I don't," Tess answered.

"My grandfather was a great fisherman. He tried to teach me, but I was never interested or good at it. Besides, the only fish we have in downtown Boston are some goldfish that swim in the fountains at the market square."

We both laughed.

"Well, Jake and I should be heading home. I mean going back to Grams. We have the Goat to climb, and we would like to get to the top before dusk. It was very nice to meet you, and by the way Jake greeted you, I would say he was quite happy to have bumped into you."

"Same here, Tess." He started to leave, but unexpectedly stopped and turned toward us.

"Tess, would you like a ride to the top of the canyon? My truck is parked at the fishing access."

Before she could answer, he continued.

"By the way, it's getting around supper time anyway, and I'm going to be stopping at the Herron diner for a home-cooked meal before heading home. Their hot roast beef sandwiches are still the best. Would you like to join me?"

Tess hesitated. She sure was hungry and not really looking forward to the climb back to the car. Besides, Jake was already panting. She could remember how delicious those hot roast beef sandwiches were, especially with french fries and gravy. She would always order that when Gram and Gramps brought her there.

"Well, I am hungry," she said.

Jake perked up when he heard the word, hungry. Gram taught him words like, 'hungry' and 'eat.'

"Hungry yet, Jake?" She would say, and then follow the words by putting a full dinner bowl of food down in front of him.

"That sounds great, Luke, if I'm not intruding. I sure could use the ride, the company, and the food," I said.

Jake made a wide circle around his mouth with his tongue.

"Did your Gram ever tell you that Jake loves the hamburgers from the diner?" Luke asked, smiling.

"I found out that secret when your Gram brought Jake in for a checkup, and I found him a little overweight. She blamed it on the Herron burger."

We both laughed as he led us back to the stream access and his white Silverado. Even Jake seemed to have a smile on his face.

"Jake can ride in the cab, and I'll move all my fishing things from the front seat and help you climb in."

I waited as he tossed the gear in the bed of the truck, and then politely offered his hand to boost me up on the running board, and safely into the passenger seat. We drove into the town of Herron and parked in front of the one and only diner in town. The small yellow and silver eatery with red and white awnings brought back such great memories for me.

"Okay Jake, you wait here, and I promise we will bring you a hamburger back," said Luke, as he helped me out of the truck.

In the diner, he ignored the sign that said, 'wait to be seated,' and I followed Luke to the last booth in the back.

"I haven't been here in such a long, long, time," I sighed and took a deep breath. "Gramps and Gram always brought me here when I was growing up. It was one of their favorite places to eat."

We opened the plastic covered menus, and both of us decided on the diner special.

"Hi Vivian," said Luke, as the waitress approached our table.

As aways, she reprimanded Luke for not following the diner rules and seating himself. Then she gave him a big smile.

"I'll try to remember next time, Viv," he said, "but for now, we will have two hot roast beef sandwiches, fries with gravy, and two cups of coffee, please. Oh yes, and a Herron burger to go. Thanks Viv."

"Coming right up, Luke," Viv said, as she smiled and shook her head.

She returned the menus to the silver clip against the wall of the booth. I didn't remember our waitress, although Luke said that she covered the second shift at the diner for years. Always blunt and sassy, Viv knew her job like the back of her hand.

"This is my usual routine when I come to Herron fishing, and I'm glad you stopped for a bite to eat with me," Luke said, as he poured some cream from the small silver pitcher into our coffee.

"So tell me about you, and what your plans are when you leave Hopewell," he said.

"Not much to tell, Luke. My mom and I moved from Abington to live with my Gram and Gramps when my father died. I was eight. After two years, my mom got sick and she died. Gram and Gramps raised me. They were so good to me and taught me a lot. In my Gram's mind, it was particularly important to be an excellent student, and going to college was a necessity when I finished high school. I applied to different universities and was accepted at Boston College. I fell in love with the big city and, after graduation, I made my home there. I'm a journalist by trade, and I spend my life traveling and covering stories for the Boston Times. In my spare time, I'm a contributing editor for some magazines. I also penned a few books. After I leave here, I'll pick up where I left off. Writing is my life. Now about you, Luke, how did you get here?"

"Well, I think it was just the opposite with me. I was born and raised in New York City. My father was a doctor, and my mother was a teacher. I went to New York City University and took up premed because I thought I wanted to follow in my dad's footsteps.

When I was still a youngster, my father would take me to the office with him in the summer and give me small jobs to do. He was the neighborhood doctor. He treated patients in the office, and he also made house calls. Sometimes I would go with him, sit on his patient's front steps, and wait for him to finish. One of his patients was an older woman, Ethel, who had a fat, tabby cat named Harvey. I would play with Harvey, eat cookies, and wait for my father, who was checking on Ethel's blood pressure and giving her instructions on her medication. There was a personal touch and healing to medicine back then. Well, anyway, Ethel was getting older and sicker, and she made my father promise to take care of Harvey after she passed. When she died, Harvey came to live with us. I genuinely loved that cat, and we became inseparable. He lived to be twenty years old, and he died just before I finished high school. I think Harvey is the one that finally influenced me to become an animal doctor. In my junior year of college, I decided to change my course of study from medical doctor to veterinarian."

Our food was served, and it looked delicious.

"I haven't had one of these in a long time," I said, cutting into the soft bread and beef, as the dark brown gravy ran into the deep cut. After we finished our dinner and ordered custard pie for dessert, we continued our talk.

"How did you make your way from New York City to Hopewell?"

"Good question, Tess. I'm asked that a lot, and my answer is that I fell in love with a black pot belly pig named Lucy." Tess looked surprised, and did not know whether to laugh or not. She did not want to be rude.

"That's okay, Tess, I get the same reaction every time I tell the story. People think I'm talking about a girl that I met and married, but since I never had a wife, I didn't have to worry about the story getting back to her. I was doing a veterinary internship at an exclusive dog and cat clinic in New York City. Very wealthy people brought their animals there to be treated and groomed. It was called, the 'Diamond Collar Pet Hospital.' Anyway, I was working the evening shift one Thursday night, and a woman rushed in with this black pot belly pig. The front desk receptionist was so upset with what she saw, that she came into my office to get me. I escorted Erma, the woman, and Lucy, the pig, back to an examining room. Erma was visibly upset. She told me the story about Lucy and her traveling by minivan from Pennsylvania to New York City to visit her sick uncle. When Lucy got out of the van, she started acting very strange. She was snorting and carrying on in a very peculiar manner."

"She didn't sleep last night, Doc," Erma said, "and this morning she did not eat, and she continued with this crazy behavior. I just can't settle her, Doc, and I am really getting worried. She was never like this before."

I tried to calm Erma, as Lucy continued pacing back and forth in the exam room. Her plump, black, round belly was almost dragging on the floor.

"I'd like to get some history first, Erma, I stated. "If you can give me some background on Lucy, I think we can begin to understand what may be bothering her."

Erma began by telling me that they were from a small town in Pennsylvania called Forrest Glen. She said that she bought Lucy when the pig was six weeks old, and she has been with her for four years. The Vet would come to see her once a year, and she never had any problems until this trip. Since Erma was going to stay here for a while and take care of her uncle, she thought she would bring Lucy with her.

"May I have the telephone number of Lucy's doctor?" I asked Erma.

"Sure Doc, here it is."

She handed me her worn red phone book and opened it to the page with 'The Country Vet' name and number on it. Anyway, after a phone call, and a discussion with Dr. Hays, we concluded that Lucy, who never traveled before, was stressed out from the change in her environment. I gave Lucy a shot of Valium, and instructed Erma to follow up with one pill of the same medication every six hours for the next two days.

"By then Lucy should be use to her new environment," I told her.

Erma was so grateful as she and her pot belly pig proudly left the clinic.

"Well, Tess, the happenings of that evening left a lasting impression on me as I continued my daily work of taking care of dogs and cats that lived like aristocrats. I wasn't a complete hotshot Vet, but I was going in that direction," he said with a smile on his face. "Given the opportunity, humility will sneak up on you when you least expect it. Anyway, weeks past and the visit from Erma and Lucy

Lucy

haunted me every day since they were there. I began to do some serious thinking about being an animal doctor. I remembered that night when Lucy needed help, and I called Dr. Hays, I didn't get an answering machine. He pleasantly answered the phone call, probably after an extremely busy day of treating all kinds of animals at his office. I knew that I wanted to be just like him. After my internship, I searched small towns that needed a Veterinarian, and I got a response from Dr. Shell from the community of Hopewell. He was getting ready to retire, and was hoping and praying that he would get a letter just like the one I sent to him. The rest is history. I moved to Hopewell and worked with Dr. Shell for about a year, and then I bought his practice. I have been here ever since. I just turned sixty last month, and I never once regretted my decision."

"It sounds like you came to Hopewell just as I was leaving for college in Boston," Tess said, finishing up her coffee.

Viv had a sixth sense about her customers taking the last sip of coffee, and she was at our booth immediately.

"Can I pour you another?" Viv asked.

"No, thank you. I had enough, and it was delicious." Tess said.

Viv went back to the counter and returned to the table with a brown paper bag that contained Jake's Herron burger.

"I see you are feeding one of your animal friends again," Viv said, as she handed the bag and the bill to Luke.

She smiled at him and quickly moved to the next booth to get the order from two new customers that just sat down. Luke paid the bill at the cash register, and he took a fresh toothpick from the container and placed it in the right corner of his mouth. With a quick wave to Viv, he and Tess left the diner, got back in the truck, and headed for the lot where Tess parked her car. Jake's nose was twitching rapidly when he got a whiff of the hamburger.

"You will have supper when you get home, Jake." Tess said, putting the bag in her purse. They drove back to the canyon and caught a glimpse of a brilliant sunset. The silence in the truck confirmed their mutual admiration and gratitude for this wonder of nature. As they rounded the bend, the sunlight reflected off the glass, and Luke instinctively pulled down his visor. A small square card fell to the floor. Tess bent over and picked it up. She stared at it. She looked out the window to confirm that the picture she was holding looked exactly like the beautiful sunset in front of them.

"Luke," she said, "where did you get this picture?"

"What picture?" he said.

He took his eyes off the road for a second to look at the card that she was holding.

"Oh gosh, I totally forgot I had that. It is a picture that your grandmother gave me. She borrowed my camera about a month before she got sick. She said that she wanted to get a clear picture of what she thought was the most beautiful sunset in the world. She took it while standing at her Springhouse, as the sun was setting over the mountain. To thank me, she had a copy of the picture made, and she gave it to me when she returned the camera. I must have clipped it behind the visor and forgotten about it. Please take that with you. It is one of the last things that your Gram did, and I would love for you to take it with you."

"She gave it to you," Tess said.

"Yes, she did, and now I am giving it to you," Luke replied.

We got to my car and Luke helped me out. Jake jumped out of the back seat.

"It was my pleasure to meet you and have dinner with you, Tess," Luke said. "Remember to call the office, and I will give Jake his exam before you leave."

"Thanks, Luke, for all of your kindness. It was a pleasure to meet you too. Jake and I will see you before we leave," I said, extending my hand to shake his. "Also, thank you so much for this picture. It means a lot to me because Gram took it herself, and because you gave it to me."

Luke shook my hand and patted Jake on the head. He climbed back in his truck and drove behind us until he reached the intersection. We took a left toward the highway, and he turned right heading home on the back roads.

When we returned home, Jake was anxious for his hamburger and gulped it down. I took a quick shower and sat down by the fire. I placed the picture that Luke gave me on the side table next to my chair, and I picked up a book that I started to read when I first arrived at Grams. It was a habit. I always liked to read for about an hour before going to sleep. After reading four chapters, I started getting tired. I reached for my book mark that I thought I placed on my lap, but it was nowhere in sight. I'll find it tomorrow, I thought, but for the time being, I'll use Gram's sunset photo. Placing it in the book, I wondered if Gram autographed and dated the back of the picture as she usually did when she gave one away. I was stunned when I saw what Gram wrote to Luke.

The world is full wonder, each time a new sun breaks
It leaves us with a story, as the moon and owl awake
The story is a message, for the open heart to take
The world is full wonder, each time a new sun breaks

Day Six

The dark Italian roast coffee tasted delicious this morning, especially since I made it in the old silver percolator that Gram used ever since I could remember. Making coffee at Gram's took more time than preparing it at home. There was something ritualistic about turning the wooden grinder, and pouring the crushed beans into the round compartment above a pot of cold spring water. Placing it on the stove and turning up the heat, one could smell the aroma as the boiling water gushed up into the glass knob, came down through the grounds, and miraculously returned to the pot as delicious coffee.

Gramps would say that Gram must 'pray over those beans or somethin' to make such good coffee. I remember that he would get up about five in the morning, break off a chunk of homemade black bread, and sit down at the kitchen table. Gram would pour him a cup of coffee in his white round mug, and he would gratefully bow his head to God and Gram.

My morning schedule in Boston was remarkably different, right down to the mechanical, automatic coffee maker that I used for its preparation. The programmed robot worked on its own, and it had a stainless steel 'to go' cup filled and waiting for me to grab on my way out the door to work.

"Come on, Jake, let's head out to the field." I said.
Jake hesitated and looked at me. He was probably trying to tell me that it was too cold, or that he was too tired, I thought. It was only 7am, but for some reason I felt energized and ready to take on the day. I put on the warm sweater that Gram had knitted for me. She made it from the wool of the sheep in the farm nearby. Gram's friend, Susan, from Goodview Farms, raised her own sheep. She sheared them, collected the wool, and spun it into spools. She

belonged to the 'Sheep to Shawl' group, and one day she gave some wool to Gram. Of course, instead of making something for herself, Gram knitted me a sweater for Christmas when I was in my first year of college. Thoughtlessly, I left it behind when I went back to school, and I found it in her room when I was going through her things. She wrapped it up in tissue paper and placed it back in the box, never saying one word to me about forgetting it. As I slipped into it, I felt awful that I neglected such a beautiful gift, and Gram's hard work.

"I bet if we could hear these walls talk, Jake, I would know how disappointed Gram felt," I said, "but I don't think even these walls would have ever seen those private and proud eyes cry."

I filled Gramps old white mug with black coffee, and Jake and I went outside. The air was crisp. The unexpected snow and ice storm a few days ago, and the unseasonably warm temperatures from yesterday, provided us today with a refreshing breeze, and the promise of spring. I thought about the beautiful day I had yesterday in Herron, and, oh yes, meeting Luke was a surprise.

I knew many men in Boston. Some real close friends, some dinner dates, but none that I wanted to be with for the rest of my life. I worked with highly ambitious people, and the sobering truth was that I was one of them. My goal was fame and fortune. People in Hopewell seemed different. Luke seemed different. Even though my time with him yesterday was brief, I was left with the impression that his life was not all about him, rather about the people he served, and the animals he helped. He seemed to be a humble man, and Jake seemed to like him a lot. Gram would always tell me that if animals and children like someone, then it is a reasonable bet that you are looking at a good person. I wanted to remember to call him today and ask him to come to dinner here on Saturday. He was so generous to me and Jake. I wanted to say thank you to him before I left town.

The weeds were up to my ankles. The field certainly needed mowing. I guess I never realized all the work Gram did to keep the farm in good shape. Walking through the field, I thought about how infrequently I asked Gram if she needed any help when I made my whirlwind visits home to see her. The mouthful of coffee washed the lump away in my throat, but the sense of regret remained.

"I guess one reason that loved ones die, Jake, is to let us know how much they mean to us," I said.

We sat down at the end of the field. I chose my little chair, and Jake sat on the ground next to me. A few squirrels chased each other in the woods behind us.

"Have you lost your urge to chase things, Jake, or is it just too early?" I questioned.

Again, Jake just looked at me.

It was a real treat for me to enjoy a leisurely morning like this. At home, I was always in a hurry, or rushing to meet a deadline. I knew running this farm was never an easy job, but the nature of it was different from the pace of my day. Generations of my family have called this place their home, and they have paved the way for me with their strength of the spirit, love, and courage. Years ago, families would never think of selling the homestead where they labored so long and hard. What would they think if they knew I was getting ready to sell it? I thought.

"Things change," I blurted out loud, trying to rationalize my thoughts and convince myself that I was doing the right thing. "Today we have more choices," I continued. "There are more opportunities to relocate and live a different life. Through the years, generations have changed the definition of what is right, and what is wrong, so I should no longer feel guilty about not keeping the farm. Honestly, coming back to all of this would be more than I could handle. I know that I am making a smart decision. I'm just being a little sentimental today, that's all. I will put all this behind me and move ahead with my plans in a few days."

Feeling anxious and blaming it on the coffee, I was no longer finding any comfort in the field. I got up from the bench and started walking toward the house. As I reached the barn, I noticed the electric candle in my old bedroom window blinking a few times and then going out. This must be an omen for me to head up to that room today and pack the rest of my things, I thought.

With boxes in one hand, and a new light bulb in the other, I headed up to the second floor.

When I was growing up, my bedroom was near Gram's room. Two stairways in the house led to the second floor, one from the kitchen, and the traditional one from the parlor. Either stairway led to a narrow hallway with the original wide plank flooring that Gram protected with brown, flowered, area rugs. An old rag doll with braids sat on a chair next to Gram's RCA Victrola that was made by the Victor Talking Machine Company in 1937. Gramps gave it to Gram so she could play her favorite records. She would give it a few cranks and move the stainless steel playing arm onto the black vinyl record that sat on a green velvet turntable. Bing Crosby would sing 'White Christmas,' not only during the holidays, but anytime Gram wanted to hear him. When the Victrola was not in use, a crocheted coverlet, and a rose beaded glass Victorian lamp rested on the closed lid.

The hallway walls held pictures of all our ancestors that probably dated back to around 1800. Gram's room was to the left, and my room was to the right. They were separated by a hand carved, decorated door. When I was young, the door always stayed open. Then as I got older, I began closing it more often when I was in my room. Gram sensed my need for privacy and never said a word.

My bedroom was small but cozy, and the best part was it belonged to me. Tan wallpaper with little bouquets of purple, gold, and green flowers throughout, covered the walls. The two window frames matched a shade of purple in the wall paper, and delicate ivory lace curtains adorned the windows.

My bed was close to the wall, and a chest of drawers and a wardrobe, which contained my clothing, was on the other side of the room. Since there were no built-in closets in the bedrooms, Gram stored the off-season clothes in the attic.

Gram's Victrola

Tess's Room

My little rocking chair with a brown teddy bear sitting on it, occupied one corner, and my roll-top desk filled the other corner. A picture of my mom, dad, and me hung on the wall, and one of Gram, Gramps, and me sat next to the brass lamp on my desk. A full length old Victorian mirror, stood by the door. It was gold plated with a hand carved, ornate design, and had been in our family for generations. It belonged to my great grandmother, and Gram wanted me to keep it in my room, so I did. I remember I would stand in front of it when I was sixteen and get ready to go to a dance. At that time, I was five foot one, weighed about a hundred pounds, and had beautiful long, brown hair.

From the doorway, the mirror caught my reflection.

Forty years brought some real changes, I thought. I was still five foot one. The light brown hair was short and highlighted to hide some gray, and I gained twenty-nine extra pounds.

"You put on some years and pounds, Tess, but you still look okay," I said out loud, as I stood there in my jeans and white blouse.

For a second, I wondered why things ever had to change. Over the years, life was perfect on this beautiful farm, and in this comfortable room.

I sat down on the ivory chenille bedspread. Gram put this one on my bed in the winter, and in the summer, she changed it to a blue and white flowered seersucker one that she made for me.

I remember those lovely summer nights when I would lay in my bed with the windows open and feel the cool night breeze. I could hear the symphony of night sounds coming from the field and the woods. The peepers, the hoot owl, and the crickets, along with the bubbling water from the stream, all entertained me as I waited for sleep to come. I loved to hear the train approaching on the railroad track that ran behind the old mill across the road. I remember I would wait for the whistle to blow, and then listen to the train wheels clicking against the iron track. After that, I would fall soundly asleep.

When I was small, my Gramps and I would cross over the same railroad tracks on our way up the mountain to pick huckleberries. He knew a spot that had the best berry bushes around.

"Come on, little one," he would say, handing me a small gray tin bucket. "Gram is in the mood to bake us some sweet huckleberry pie." Gram would smile and nod her head.

"Take good care of her up there, Gramps," she reminded him. When we returned, Gram and I washed and cleaned the berries. After putting some aside for Mrs. Como, she would always freeze a pint or two depending on how much we brought back.

"Always remember to share a portion of what you have," she said. "Be open to receiving as well. You don't want to take the gift away from the giver."

Gram baked the best huckleberry pie I ever tasted. I was never sure if it was a secret recipe, or rather all the love and time she put into it.

I walked over to the window that faced the back of the house and pulled the curtain aside. Looking down, I could see the stone path, and the brown cone flower stems with their dried seed heads. Gram never cut them down in the fall. She liked to keep them up throughout the winter so that the yellow finches could perch on the tips and eat the seeds, and the first snow would fill the empty heads.

I longed for Gram and my entire family tonight, and the longing haunted me. I had the urge to remember the time in my life that was simple and beautiful. As I stood by my window, the memories rolled past like an animated slide show and entertained me.

When I was a young girl, I would dress in my best holiday clothes. I watched from this window as our family and friends arrived for a tasty dinner and a holiday celebration.

Gram's Coneflowers

Thanksgiving and Christmas were extra special holidays for me because that was the time when everyone came to our house. Gram and Gramps started that tradition a long time ago, and since then, it was the family gathering place every year. As each car came up our road and parked alongside the barn, I watched as everyone headed into our house. The parlor was the room where all of our Christmas and Thanksgiving celebrations began.

What a feast Gram would prepare for us. There was a certain contentment knowing that Gram was in the kitchen making our favorite meal. At Christmas, Gram would set the table with candles, a holly and bayberry centerpiece, and she would place a sprig of rosemary in each our cloth napkins. She would cook delicious food. We ate turkey, ham, and roast beef with side dishes of buttered carrots and yams glazed in maple syrup and brown sugar. My favorite was fresh green beans topped with almonds and bacon bits. Gram would make her favorite potato stuffing and homemade bread. After dinner, we would all gather around the Christmas tree, and open presents. No matter how modest the parlor, the bubbling candle lights on the tree instantly transformed it into a magnificent, magical place. We received wonderful gifts that were either handmade, or inexpensively bought at J.J.Newberry. Mouthwatering scents from Gram's fresh baked pies, cookies, pieces of homemade chocolates, and ribbon candy announced that desserts were about to be served. Everyone would say that they could not eat another bite, but we all managed to fit in a little bit more. Then the men went to watch TV, and the women remained at the table to talk, drink Gram's Italian coffee, and eat her homemade cranberry and walnut biscotti. All of us kids either played games, or if it snowed, went outside to build snowmen. At the end of the evening, no one wanted to say good-bye, but there was always the promise of visiting soon again. Still looking out the window, I could almost hear the snow crunch under their feet as they made their way out the door and back to their cars.

The Christmas Tree

For a moment, I was aware of the shared joy and comfort that we all felt on those holidays. Thank you Gram, I thought, for your steadfast influence in honoring tradition. Thank you for giving us the opportunity for the hugs, kisses, and laughter. Thank you for teaching us the importance and the true meaning of family.

My cell phone rang stirring me from my reflection. I answered it on the third ring. It was my supervisor from the Boston Times. After exchanging some conversation about how I was doing, and how things were going, he asked if I planned to return Monday.

"I'm glad you called Jim. I have been so busy and preoccupied here, I didn't even realize that a week has gone by. I'm sorry to say that I will not be returning Monday. I plan to take another week, so I guess I will be seeing you the following Monday. I hope that will be okay?"

"Sure, Tess, everyone here misses you, and we all hope that you are doing well. If there is anything you need, give us a call."

"Thanks, Jim, bye."

"Bye, Tess."

I hung up the phone from Jim, and decided to give Luke a call. After retrieving his card from my purse, I dialed his office number at the animal clinic. It rang a few times, and then his answering machine picked up.

"This is Luke LeFevre. If this is an emergency, please dial zero. Otherwise, please leave your name and phone number, and I will return your call as soon as possible."

After the beep, I left my message.

"Hi Luke, this is Tess. I thought I would call and invite you to dinner on Saturday evening. I know it may be short notice, but I am only in town for one more week, and I want to thank you for your kindness by making you dinner. Give me a call when you have time. My number is 484-553-0631. Thanks."

I hung up the phone, and smiled. Then I decided to go through the box of books sitting next to my desk.

When Gram felt good, she was an avid reader. Her favorite was non-fiction and autobiographies. Gram visited the library often, and chose her books from there, or she would take a bus into the city and buy them at a small family-owned bookstore. Sometimes, when she was in Herron, she would have Gramps drop her off at the 'Relax and Read' bookstore, while he went fishing for the day, and he would pick her up when he finished. The store had a section with three comfortable, easy chairs for customers to enjoy reading in the store, if they wished.

"I don't know how you can spend the whole day reading and shopping," he would say to her, "but whatever makes you happy, and of course gives me time to fish, works for me."

When Gram was finished with her books, she would ask Mrs. Como if she wanted to read them. The ones she did not want, Gram would donate to the library. That was one of her weekly stops. Louise, the head librarian, knew Gram very well.

Louise and I went to school together, and Gram would take Louise and I to the reading circles at the library when we were children. When mom and I came to live with Gram, mom transferred me into the second grade at Hopewell Elementary, and that is where I met Louise. We became close friends over the years, playing together in grade school and going to dances and malt shops in high school. We both loved reading and writing, and both of us loved our after school and summer jobs. Louise worked at the library, and I worked at the Hopewell Chronicle, the newspaper in our little town. When we graduated, we both chose to follow our passion. I wanted very much to go to school in New England and become a journalist, while Louise had a strong desire to head for Colorado to become a librarian. We'd exchange letters and see each other when we came home on school breaks. She returned to Hopewell after she earned her doctorate in library science. She married Steven, a dentist in town, and had two boys, who are married and have children of their own. One is a small courts judge in New York City, and the other, a physical therapist in Herron.

"I think I'll take these books to the library today," I said out loud.

There wasn't much more to do in this room. The only things that I wanted to take with me were the mirror, the desk, and my little rocker. I would have the moving company pack up those items. Besides, I wanted to see some of the old places from my childhood and take some notes for my journal.

The library will be perfect, and it will give me a chance to see Louise again, I thought. With Gram gone and the farm sold, I did not know when I would be back to Hopewell. I carried the box of books down the creaky old stairway that led to the parlor, and out to my car.

"Stay here and guard the house, Jake, I won't be long."

Hoping Louise would be working today, I headed to the Library.

The Hopewell Library was on the main street, and Louise was busy checking out a book for a reader when I arrived. She turned quickly just to see who was coming through the door, smiled, then turned back to the customer to hand them the stamped book, and wish them a good day. As quickly as her legs could carry her, she walked from behind the wooden counter and directly toward me. She removed her black framed glasses, allowing them to dangle from the crocheted holder around her neck.

"Oh, my gracious God, Tess! Tess, how delightful to see you," she said.

She took the box of books from my hands, placed them on the counter, and stretched her arms out to hug me. I gave her a big hug too.

"Hello Louise, I was hoping you would be here. It is so good to see you too," I said.

"I came to the cemetery for the service," Louise said, "but I stayed in the back."

The Hopewell Library

"I'm not very good with words at a time like that. I loved your Gram so much. She would come in sometimes two, three times a week. I would try to take my break when she was here, and we would slip over to the diner for some coffee. She was a good friend. How have you been through all of this?" She asked.

"I've been okay. I'm thankful that I was able to be with her before she died, and I'm also grateful that she did not suffer, I answered. "I know that she is happy with her God and her family in Heaven. That was one thing about my Gram, she was never afraid of dying. I'm staying at the farm while I take care of things, and every day there is something that always reminds me of the way life use to be when I lived there. I miss her so much."

"Well, when you move into the house again, you will be surrounded by all that she loved. I hope to be see you more often." Louise said, squeezing my hand.

"Oh, Louise, I know that if I were moving back that would be true, but I am in the process of trying to find a buyer for the farm. I hope to find someone that will take very good care of it. I will be going back to Boston in about a week. I really need to get back to work. Anyway, that is why I stopped in today. I wanted to see you and thank you for everything, and to bring you some books that Gram was getting ready to bring to the library herself," I said.

"How is the family?" I asked, trying to change the subject.

"They are just wonderful, Tess. They keep us busy, but we love it. I think Steven is going to retire in about two years, and then we may do some traveling. I know you travel to some great places with your job, so maybe I will call you for some pointers when we are ready to go. By the way, you look great."

"You too, Louise," I said.

Louise was always attractive. About five three and very slender, she looked about the same as she did in college. She had beautiful long black hair, and she wore it up in a twist or a bun. I could see some gray along her hair line, and we both added some thin lines around our mouths and eyes.

"I should be on my way," I said. "Maybe the next time I'm in town, we can have lunch and catch up. I'll call first. Take care and say hi to the family for me."

"You too," she said, and I'll hold you to that lunch." We both gave each other a hug, but as I turned to go, she stopped me.

"Tess, before you leave, can you do me one favor?" she asked.

"Sure Louise, you name it," I said.

"Can you go back to the local author's section, pull out your Gram's book, and on the page where she signed it, write the date that she died? I could do it, but it would be very special to me if you would do it," she said.

I hope I didn't look too surprised when she said 'Gram's Book.' At that moment, I was so grateful that she was called back to the desk to help a customer before she discovered the shocked look on my face.

Book? What book? Gram wrote a book? I said to myself, as I walked to the back of the library, and to the local author's section where Louise directed me. I knew that Gram had a journal in her dresser, but that was just filled with notes that she jotted down throughout the years. When I was a child, I watched her write in that book. One time I asked her what she was writing. Now, I remember her words.

"Oh, Tess, maybe someday I'll write a book."

That was her one and only response to me. I never asked again, and she never said anything more about it. Now, I was standing in front of a hard cover, black book with the title done in an exquisite gold calligraphy.

POEMS AND PROSE
BY
ANGELINE ORLANDO

My hand shook as I reached for the book. I walked into one of the two private reading booths, so I could be alone. I slowly opened Gram's book. Inside the cover was the date it was published by the Morris publishing company, and an ISBN number confirming its entry into the Library of Congress. The dedication page read:

To Tess,
For all that you are, and all that you do

The next page displayed an author's note:

May the undying Presence that surrounds this book, follow me through these pages. May the ideas that are above, below, and around me flow through me, and become alive through the written word. I ask that the possibilities that are only available to those whose reach is far beyond their grasp, be given to this writer's outstretched hands.

My God, when did she write this? I thought. The publishing date was 1978. That was the year that I started my career in Boston. I could feel the tears filling my eyes. The words arrogant and self consumed repeatedly came to mind. In those years, life was all about me. It was all about what I was doing, and writing, and accomplishing. Gram would sit and listen to me go on and on about myself when I would visit. Every conversation concerned itself with me, and nothing else. I underestimated Gram's feelings. How imperfect my view.

Holding her book became powerfully compelling as I began to understand what she already understood back then. Gram, who had little formal education, in this moment, became the greatest teacher I ever had.

I began to page through the book. It was filled with beautiful poems and short stories about life, and beauty, and love that I could not begin to capture in my writing. As I got to last page, the penmanship changed, highlighting a piece of prose. It was done in the same gold calligraphy that appeared on the cover of the book. Gram always connected the color gold to wisdom, and wisdom to the mind, and the mind to knowledge, and knowledge to understanding.

"What is it Gram," I whispered, "what are you trying to tell me?"

I remembered Mrs. Como's words.

"Precious signs come when we least expect them, Tess," she said. "We must hope that we do not miss them."

Gram ended her book with a piece of prose that was distinctive and exclusive from the rest of her writing. This had to be a sign. This had to be important. I desperately wanted to know her meaning.

"Yes, we must hope that we do not miss it." I sighed.

With my trembling hand on the page, and my eyes filled with tears, I began to read slowly and carefully the words of my personal and unsung hero, my Gram.

The Beauty of the Evening

In the beauty of the evening, comes the memory of the day
in the silence of the night, as we bow our heads and pray
we remember all the footsteps, of our path along the way
in the beauty of the evening, comes the memory of the day

In the living of our life, the joys and sorrows that we know
in the dying of the body, comes the unveiling of the soul
we lay our heads softly, in the arms that won't let go
in the dying of the body, comes the unveiling of the soul

Oh we celebrate our coming, when we hear a new born cry
we agonize our leaving, with a strained and painful sigh
the spirit soars the heavens, and renews itself on high
again we celebrate our coming, as we hear a new born cry

I know you are my brother, for I've helped you once before
I carried you to shelter, and laid my back against the door
for when the storm was over, I walked with you once more
I know you are my brother, for I've helped you once before

You stretched your hand out to me when others went away
I needed arms to comfort, and I needed hands to pray
and there you stayed with me, 'till I saw the light of day
You stretched your hand out to me when others went away

When we hold our hands together, we create a symphony
and the music that emerges, is the sound of you and me

we sing it oh so softly, yet it echoes in the breeze
when we hold our hands together, we create a symphony

You will feel His comfort, on a night you search for rest
you will feel His loving presence, on a day you call you best
from the infant in the cradle, to the elder on death's bed
you will feel his peace, on a night you search for rest

We hear roar of the mighty river, the trickle of the stream
flight of the soaring eagle, the gliding hawk on wing
Aware that the mighty spirit, inspires the human dream
the roar of the mighty river, lifts the gliding hawk on wing

Oh! little caterpillar, oh! gracious butterfly
one clings to the earth, and the other to the sky
we need to learn to walk first, before we learn to fly
oh! little caterpillar, oh! gracious butterfly

Then, as I began to read the last verse, I was taken aback by the familiarity of the words. Since Gram's death, I had been finding these words everywhere.

The world is full wonder, each time a new sun breaks
it leaves us with a story, as the moon and owl awake
the story is a message, for the open heart to take
the world is full wonder, each time a new sun breaks

Could it be a coincidence? maybe. Eye tricks? perhaps. Why the same message, over and over again? Why didn't Gram tell me about her book? Why did she dedicate it to me? Why didn't she give me a copy? I wrote the date of Gram's birth and death under her signature, closed the book, and replaced it on the shelf where it belonged. I wanted to ask Louise if I could have it, but in my heart I knew that I had no right to its ownership. I had not earned it.

As I passed the front desk, Louise was still busy with some customers. She turned as I passed. We waved to each other and smiled. I left the library terribly confused.

102

Day Seven

Another beautiful day appeared this morning, and somehow I was glad that I had one more week here. Just a few days ago, I was in a hurry to return to the city. This morning, as I sat at the kitchen table with Jake at my feet and drank my coffee, I did not feel the urge to be anywhere else but in this house, and on this farm.

Gram's book haunted me. Last night when I got home, I searched the bookshelves in the parlor to see if she placed a copy of her book there. It was nowhere to be found.

Gram had such wisdom and humility, I thought. It seemed as if she lived in two realms that were both parallel to each other. One was the human body which was physical, essential and real. It was necessary to fulfill her daily responsibilities, and care for herself, Gramps, me, and the people she loved. Then there was the other self, perhaps a higher self, who lived apart from the everyday judgments, opinions, and criticisms of others. This self was the one that the human hand could not touch or harm, and of which the human opinion did not matter. This spirit lived solely to strive for a perfection that was unattainable on this earth, only to be realized after the human life was irrelevant.

I walked to the window to look at the birds perched on the feeder, trying to gather the last seeds that Gram had put in there before she died. Gram always made sure that her friends always had enough seeds, and a block of homemade peanut butter suet to eat.

Today, I wanted to take the time to see what was left in the barn, Gramps workshop, and the summer kitchen. I knew most of the things that were there would be going to the auction that the realtor would arrange, but I still wanted to walk through the old buildings one more time.

"Come on, Jake, let's go investigate," I said.

I put on some old clothes, tied a scarf around my head, and out we went.

Gram's Barn

Gram's Herb Garden

The barn was across the road to the right side of the house. Pulling open the heavy doors, I entered from the back. I stood on the top floor of the barn and looked up at the high rafters constructed a long time ago from strong oak trees. There were a few pigeons staring down at my intrusion, and they seemed as if they were questioning my visit. To my right and left were thick stone walls, with narrow slits chiseled into the rocks. The other two walls were constructed from wood.

With the use of stone masons, my ancestors built this barn in 1838. Gram told me that her great-great grandfather patched a red clay mariner's compass into the stone at the peak of the barn because he was so proud of his accomplishment. The compass faced the house, and he imprinted his name and the date within the circle.

The bays to the right and left were empty. Some of the wide, thick floor boards were decayed, and even absent in some places. The central bay was intact, and Gramps old red fishing canoe and paddles were sitting there. He turned it upside down and placed it on two wooden horses each time he returned from his fishing trips in Herron. The last trip was a long time ago, and the thick covering of cobwebs and dust gave evidence to that truth. I felt sad to see that it lay dormant for so long, but it sure made a wonderful man happy during his lifetime.

The creaks and squeaks throughout the barn reminded me of my childhood days, especially Halloween. The barn had no electricity, and the mystery of its ominous darkness hid the terrors that could be lurking in its deep shadows. It was a perfect place to assume that ghosts and goblins roamed freely there. It was a good hiding spot when Gramps use to play hide and seek with me, until I became so scarred and ran out on my own. Gramps would laugh and tell me that the ghouls were his best helpers.

He used old white sheets and poles to make ghosts in the fields, and when it came time for the full harvest moon, the glow illuminated the phantoms. The eerie sight made me and

Gram uneasy, but Gramps always assured us that he would save us from harm. Just to make sure, Gram would throw salt over her shoulder, and plant rosemary by our back door for good luck. Gramps would just smile at it all.

Then we would go into the pumpkin patch, and select three pumpkins for jack-o-lanterns. Gram would save the pulp for pies, and toast the seeds in the oven.

Those days were in the past. There is no place where time stands still, I thought, as the reality of selling Gram's farm tugged at my thoughts and lifted me out of my daydream of the past.

Using the sturdy wooden ladder, I climbed down to the lower part of the barn that was used to house the horses and livestock. The stalls were empty, with some old, stale hay lying around. The top part of the stall door would not budge. Stooping down, I was able to exit from the lower half and out into the old animal barnyard. Two stone walls were the only ones left standing. Gram found the soil here to be an excellent habitat for her herbs and perennials. Every year like clockwork, an abundant supply of herbs, chamomile, brown eyed susan, daisy, and cone flower, lifted themselves out of the earth and grew abundantly. Gram had the sundial that I gave to her as a gift one Christmas secured to a thick weathered post in the center of the herb garden.

Gramps' workshop was next, so Jake and I headed up the hill. In the distant field, I could see a group of robins starting to look for some food where the snow had melted. Some red cardinals were sitting on the forsythia branches, and a few of its yellow flowers were being persuaded to make their initial introduction.

A few snow-on-the-mountain and some early spring crocus were erupting on each side of the workshop door. As I entered, the sun, coming through the windows, lit up the shop, and I could see that everything that Gramps' used to run the farm was still in the same place. I took a deep breath and, along with the air, I inhaled the familiar old smells.

When I was a little girl, Gramps was my hero. There was nothing that he couldn't do or make in his workshop. He was a man of the land, who had a strong relationship with nature. Besides doing what needed to be done, when it needed to be done, he also helped the neighbors with gardening, farming, plowing their fields, or bundling the hay. He also enjoyed the simple things in life like making special gifts in his workshop for us and his friends. I use to think that magic happened at his workbench, and Gramps loved it when I believed that he was the magician. His enchanted wands were all the tools that he had inherited or accumulated throughout his years. The finished product was not an illusion at all, rather the accomplishment of his experienced hands, and the respect for the building block that he used. I loved to sit and watch Gramps make things. He had a chair in the shop just for me and explained what he was doing as he went along. He was extremely particular about all his measurements as he was putting things together. He taught me to hammer nails and use a screwdriver.

Although he thought that his old ways were the best, he realized that change was always in front of him, and he was open to trying new things.

"We are shaped by our opportunities," he would say to me, "even the ones we let slip by."

Gramps taught me many things, but at the top of the list, he taught me to treat people with love and respect, and to live by the Golden Rule. Gramps didn't say much, and he certainly did not explain the little that he said, so as a child, I always wondered what most of it meant. However, as I grew up and began to understand, I realized the significance of his words.

"Tess, it's important to keep going long after you can't," or "make new mistakes every day," or "you know, Tess, money is a lousy way of keeping score," he would say. Sometimes he would speak of honor.

"Tess, credentials on the wall do not necessarily make you a decent human being."

Many times, he sounded philosophical.

"Two people can look at the same thing, Tess, and see something totally different."
One time he said to me.
"You know, Tess, it seems like the people that we care about most in life are taken from us too soon."
One year after he told me that, Gramps got sick and died. I was fifteen. He was right. It was too soon.

Gramps was born in March of 1910. He was three years older than Gram. In stature he was around five foot eleven, but carried himself as if he were ten feet tall. He was smart, strong, open-minded, and a creative thinker. He was always motivated by the truth alone, and always had the strength of character to do the right thing. A very proud, honest and responsible man, he was a friend to everybody that needed one. He was part of the group that met at the diner for morning coffee, and his mug had a big 'P' on the front. He liked to be the first one there and joked about being the first to be served. Although he often got the first cup, he always made sure that everyone at the counter had one before he would allow the waitress to give him the second.
He loved animals and cared for them, and he respected their place on this earth. He and his brothers helped his parents work their farm, and provided food for themselves and the community.
Gramps met Gram at a barn dance in Hopewell in August 1930, and they got married on October 10, 1931. Because of the effects of the Depression, they had a small wedding on the front porch of the farm, and honeymooned in Herron. They loved and cared for each other. Sometimes, they would sit on the porch in the evening, and I would hide in the doorway and giggle when I saw them holding hands. They always made time for each other, if only to have a cup of tea. Gram always told me that she was grateful for all the years she shared with Gramps.
"It was a roller coaster ride some of the days," she would say, "but there were lessons learned, joys remembered, meals

shared, and nights of rest and love. What more can anyone ask for?"

Gramps was always healthy and only saw a doctor after his home remedies failed to get him better. He was doctoring for his heart when he had the attack, and he died at home in Gram's arms a few days later. He was not as spiritual as Gram, but he acknowledged and believed in a Higher Power. As he laid in bed his last few days, Gram and he would talk about the afterlife.

"We will see what is there when we cross over, Angeline," he told her, "and if there is a Place like you talk about, I will be waiting there for you."

Gram missed him so much after he died. She picked up with the farm responsibilities where he left off. When she got too old, Gram let the fields go uncultivated, and the farm became animal and crop free.

Although it had been many years since Gramps died, his tools, and his two Allis Chalmers tractors were still in the same place. The picture of Gram at eighteen, posed in a bathing suit, still hung above his workbench. My, she was so beautiful, I thought. I remember she told me that she sewed her bathing suit and was so proud to have a nice figure to show it off.

"But only to your Gramps," she would say.

Then she would go on and on about her first date with Gramps.

In the far corner sat her old sewing machine. I remembered when Gram would take me to buy bolts of fabric and let me pick out the patterns. They later became my summer clothes for play, and winter clothes for school. Some years ago, she asked the neighbor to take it out to the workshop when she was no longer able to sew. Her eyesight was getting worse, and the arthritis in her fingers made it almost impossible to operate the machine.

In the last section of the workshop was Gramps car, his 1952 Chevy. He loved that car and saved long and hard to buy it for $2,095.00. When Gram was younger, she would drive it when needed. As she got older, she gave up driving altogether, and depended on the neighbors to get her where she had to go. They never minded helping Gram, and she was always extremely generous with money, homemade baked goods, or gifts for their kindness.

I walked over to Gramps workbench. Against the back edge, there was a slat from an old green shutter with the words, 'Enjoy the moment' printed on it in white paint. A board and nails were sitting in the middle of his bench, and a hammer was lying next to the piece of wood. It looked as if Gramps had just been working there, and he walked away for a few minutes to take a break.

"I cannot see you Gramps, but I know you're here," I whispered. "Please let me know that selling the farm is the right decision. I look around, and I think of the carefree days when I called this farm my home. We lived here and enjoyed every season. The fun filled days of summer, the quiet days of autumn, and the stark days of January that turned into the blossoming days of spring. Is selling the farm the right thing to do? Am I clinging to the familiar just because it's comfortable? You know I have my life to go back to in Boston. Come on Gramps, you were always filled with such wisdom and eager to pass it on to me. I thought when people die, they are supposed to help their loved ones. Why are you making it so difficult for me? My mind and heart are open to your insight and guidance. Can't you give me just one little sign, just one?"

Jake started barking and ran to the door. His quick reaction to whatever startled him, jolted me from my whimpering, and insistent plea to Gramps. I walked to the door to see what was causing Jake such concern. Luke's white Silverado was slowly making its way up the road.

Walking out of the workshop, I waved, and he pulled up alongside the building and parked. Getting out of the truck, he walked towards me.

Gramp's Workbench

"Good morning, Tess," he said. "You too, Jake," giving him a pat on the head and a rub on his belly.

"Why, good morning, Luke," I answered in a surprised tone of voice. "What brings you around this morning?"

"I hope I'm not intruding, but I received your message yesterday about coming to dinner, and I thought I would drive by and reply in person instead of calling you," he said.

"Oh no, you are not intruding at all, Luke, I was just going through the out buildings to see what was still around. Just as I suspected, Gram didn't touch a thing," I said. "In a way I'm glad she didn't, otherwise I would have never had my trip down memory lane today. It sure did stir up some incredible memories, and for a second, I had some insane idea about keeping this old place. Good thing it didn't last very long."

"I know what you mean, Tess. These surroundings can trigger some heartwarming times," he said. "I'm sure it can be difficult."

"I guess you're right," Tess said, "but I better stop daydreaming, and start working on a plan. I have to get some order to all of this by the time I turn it over to the realtor and auctioneer next week."

The air was crisp and cool, and one single crocus was erupting from the earth that stood between us.

"Looks like spring is making a good effort today," Luke said, pointing to the little flower.

"Do you feel like a cup of coffee? I can make it as fast as Gram's old percolator will go?" Tess asked.

"No thanks, but I'll take you up on your dinner invitation for tomorrow night. I'm on my way to help one of my patients deliver her young. Nel had a difficult pregnancy, and we are hoping that she will have a healthy colt." Luke said.

"By the way, Tess, I know that your days are busy, but would you like to go to a parade on Sunday? I don't know if you remember, but Herron always has a Spring Fest celebration to welcome the coming of spring. They have an old fashioned parade as part of the festivities. I thought you may want to capture some of that before you return to the city."

"You know Luke, I would love to go. It has been forever since I saw a parade. I do remember Spring Fest. Gram and Gramps use to take me there all the time."

"Great," Luke said. "Then I will see you Saturday for dinner, and Sunday, for the parade. What time shall I be here, and what is your favorite wine?"

"Six will be fine, and please, Luke, will you choose the wine? I am serving pasta."

"That sounds great, so I will see you then," he said.

With that, he patted Jake good-bye, climbed into the truck, and disappeared down the road.

What a swell guy, I thought, and surprisingly found myself looking forward to our dinner and a parade.

I had one more out building to visit, and that was the old summer kitchen.

Built by my ancestors in1836, they lived and farmed the land from this structure until 1860 when the farm house was completed. The outer dimensions were approximately twelve feet by sixteen feet. The corners consisted of large pieces of cut limestone. The body of the two-foot-thick walls was filled with ordinary uncut field stones of various types and sizes. There were two large windows with deep sills hollowed out on each side of the house, separated by a large walk-in fireplace. The flue for the stove pipe was an empty cavity running vertically through the middle of the wall, up to the peak of a wood shake roof, and into a short, sturdy brick chimney. For cross ventilation, there was a window opening in the back wall, opposite the door. The floors were constructed from smooth beams hewed from black walnut trees that dotted the surrounding land. A narrow, winding stairway led to a small one windowed room or loft on the second floor. The ceiling was finished with lath and plaster, and the inner surfaces of the stone and mortar walls were plastered and then whitewashed. When they moved to the farmhouse, the building became a real summer kitchen which was particularly popular at that time. It provided a place to prepare meals, bake, and heat water for bathing and laundry. More important, it kept the heat of a wood-burning stove out of the house during summer months and reduced the likelihood of a farmhouse fire.

It all started here, I thought. Even though the building was in disrepair, Gram's old table and chairs were still standing in the same place. The shelves above them still held the old Ball jars that she used for canning and pickling and storing cherries. Once clear, spotless, and filled, they were now cloudy and empty from the layers of dust upon them. The floor boards were rotting in some places, and I had to be careful as I walked over to the fireplace. An old black cast iron pot hung on a hook over what use to be a source of heat for their cooking. I could just imagine lifting the lid, and finding a bubbling pot of beef stew.

Two old rockers occupied the space by the windows, and I needed to move one to climb the curved stairway that led to the second floor loft. An old rope bed and the remains of a straw mattress were in the right hand corner under the slanted part of the ceiling.

Jake began to whimper at the bottom of the steps, afraid to climb the uneven and narrow stairway.

"Just a minute, Jake," I said, "I'll be right down."

With that, I heard him drop down to a lying position in wait of my promise.

Again, I looked back at the bed, and the simplicity of my surroundings. Immediately, my thoughts raced back to my life in Boston. At night when I climbed into my soft, warm bed, all I thought about was what I managed, or did not manage to get done during the day, instead of being thankful for the comfort and warmth that it provided for me. In the morning, I hit the ground running. The last thing I thought about was giving thanks for being alive for one more day. I forgot about being grateful for the piece of toast that I gobbled down, and the cup of coffee I gulped on my way to the train. For a moment, I allowed myself to feel the difference. A feeling that I probably buried for a long time. Here on the farm, life was uncomplicated, yet complete. I felt centered, strong, and grateful here, and I wondered how driving just six hours north made me oblivious to the true wonders of life, and the day's real gifts. Where, along the fast three lane highway that leads into the big city of Boston, does this transformation take place? Then I thought, maybe there is no physical crossover on the way from here to there. Maybe nothing changes. Maybe only I change.

I started my descent down the stairs. When Jake heard me, he was up on all fours and wagging his tail.

"Gram really has you spoiled," I said. "She has me spoiled too."

I took one more look around. It will be the last time I see this place, I thought. Do I want to take anything with me as a reminder? Gramps old pipe lay on the wooden table. A red can, half full of Prince Albert tobacco, sat next to it. I decided to take that with me.

"Well, Gramps, this is it. Is there no message yet?" I said out loud. "I'm waiting."

I no sooner said the words when I thought I heard a deep voice, that sounded like my Gramps voice, trying to offer me some of his advice.

"Perhaps, Tess, you should look for your fate on the very road you took to avoid it," the voice said.

Although I was being skeptical when I asked for his help, I was scared when this voice came out of nowhere.

Enough of this craziness, I thought, as I ran out of the summer kitchen. As door slammed behind me, I turned around and, I swear, I saw Gramps standing there. He was leaning against the doorway with his one arm folded and supporting the other arm that held his pipe up to the corner of his mouth. I could smell the Price Albert tobacco as he puffed and exhaled. He was smiling from ear to ear with the same old grin that he wore when he thought he pulled one over on me or Gram.

Day Eight

Today was Saturday. I had been in Hopewell and at Grams for one week. As the song of the noisy percolator pulsed, it pushed the smell of strong coffee all through the house. I thought it was odd that the morning sky was cloudy, since the weatherman predicted another spring like day. I peeked out the kitchen door, and just as I thought, the smell of rain was in the air.

Gram loved days like today.

"An overcast day is my favorite kind of day," she would say.

Gram also loved being outdoors. When I was a little girl, I would sit by the kitchen window and watch Gram. When the snow melted in early March, and the earth was dry enough, she would hang out our freshly washed clothes and bed sheets on the clothesline. Walking back and forth, she would wipe the line clean with a dry cloth and then reach for the wooden clothespins, and her first piece of clothing to be hung. Sometimes she would raise the lines up higher with the notched wooden posts that Gramps made for her. The combination of the wet clothes, and the coolness of the March air always made her hands red and cold when she came back into the house. I could smell the scent of soap and bleach as she cupped her hands around my face so I could feel the cold. Sometimes, it turned into a game. I would run away from her, and she would chase after me.

I sat down at the kitchen table, and Jake sat at my feet on the blue and cranberry braided rug. I thought about Gram in her kitchen. Gram cooked on a coal stove most of her life. After many years, she reluctantly replaced it with a gas one. She was a fantastic cook, yet she never used a recipe. When Gramps and I saw her wrapping a scarf around her head and putting on her green flowered apron, we knew that we were going to get some mighty tasty baked goods. Our favorite was the warm cinnamon rolls that she made.

117

Gram's Kitchen

After my mom died, Gramps would come down to the elementary school every day when school let out, and walk back home with me. When we came in the kitchen door, the aroma of cinnamon captured our senses. It was coming from the fresh rolls that just came out of the oven and were cooling on the rack. Even though Gram reminded us to wait until after supper for our treat, Gramps and I would throw off our coats and seat ourselves at the kitchen table. We would sneak a roll, add creamy butter, and slowly unravel the warm spirals still cooling in our hands.

"You know Jake, I miss living here, but I know that things would not be the same if I moved back," I said as I reached down to pet him. "Now, I must really stop this reminiscing. It's all great memories of happy times, loving times, and an appreciation that I was part of it all, but those times are over. Luke is coming for supper tonight, and I need to get started preparing a meal."

I found myself saying supper instead of dinner. In Boston, I always referred to it as dinner. Perhaps the influence of the city's lifestyle made me forget the beauty and the simplicity of the word, supper.

"So supper it will be tonight, Jake," I said firmly, "but regardless of what we call it, I need to get going."

In Boston, I was always so busy working overtime during the week, that I rarely had time to prepare meals. I usually grabbed something on my way home from work.

I loved to cook, and I think mom and Gram were responsible for that. We spent so many enjoyable times in this kitchen, not only making food and eating, but hashing over the events of our day. I think the love of cooking grew out of the warm contentment I felt in this room.

First, I needed to decide what I was going to make, and then head to the grocery store for the ingredients. Good thing I asked Gram to write down some of her delicious recipes that were passed down to her by her Italian ancestors.

"Well, Tess, I don't exactly know what to write down," was her response to my request. "It's a little of this, and some of that, so I just do not know."

119

"Oh Gram," I would say, "please try to estimate what it would be in measure."

Thank God that she did the best she could with my request, because this morning I found myself being very selective. I wanted the meal to be special tonight however I convinced myself that it was for no other reason than to practice my gourmet touch, and maybe show off a little. There was nothing more to it.
Finishing my coffee, I got dressed and headed for the Hopewell Grocery store. I knew exactly where to go. The store had been in the same location ever since I could remember, and Gram always shopped there, even after a leading grocery chain opened a store on the outskirts of town. Hopewell Grocery was owned and operated by Mr. Donald Bingenzo. Everyone called him Mr. Donald for short. It was on the corner of Olive and Main Streets, and as I parked the car along the cement curb, I was amazed that the place still looked the same. A yellow-brick building supported a red and green wood canopy that protected two large glass windows on each side. On the windows, Mr. Donald advertised the weekly specials, and gave the customer a glimpse of the goodies to be bought within. It was seven thirty in the morning and there he was, Mr. Donald, just like clockwork in his clean, starched, white apron. He was sweeping the sidewalk in front of the store, and just turned the door sign from closed to open. He held an unlit Italian parody in the corner of his mouth. Mr. Donald was a man in his early seventies. He was medium height, stout, with graying hair that could be seen around the edges of his Phillies baseball cap that he wore each day.

His great grandfather, Chachi, came to America from Tuscany, Italy a long time ago and opened this market. It was passed down through the generations to his grandfather, Antonio, and then to his father. In the early 1900's, the building was more than just a grocery store. The basement was the home of a Bocce Ball court, where the men of this Italian community would gather after the store closed for the day. This ancient game, that required skill, strategy, and luck, brought friends together that enjoyed hours of playing the game downstairs. As I understand it, the old court is still in the same place, and although the Bocce balls lay dormant, and cobwebs cover the playing area, the faint smell of half smoked Italian parodies and stale wine still linger there. When his father, Louie, died in his early forties, Donald inherited the store. He was in his late twenties and had just returned from the army. He was young, thin, and had dark black hair under his Phillies cap, that he wore each day.

"Good morning, Mr. Donald," I said, sneaking up behind him.

"Oh my! Good morning, Tess," he said.

He rested the broom against the brick building and extended his arms to give me a big hug.

"I did not think I would see you after your Gram's funeral. I thought you would be back to Boston by now," he said.

"You know, Mr. Donald, you are the first person I talked to that did not think I was keeping the farm and moving back to Hopewell to live." I answered.

"Well, I have to be honest with you," he said. "I did think that you were staying, but you know how word travels fast in Hopewell. Mrs. Como was shopping here yesterday, and told me that you were selling the farm and returning to Boston,"

"Come in and visit and I can show you some of the improvements I have made in the store. I will make some espresso for us. If I remember correctly, your Gram said that you really enjoy it. I remember she would buy some espresso beans every time she knew that you were coming home," he said.

He held the door open for me, and grabbed the broom to bring back into the store. I laughed to myself because I didn't see very much that changed.

924

The Hopewell Grocery Store

The Hopewell Grocery Store

I didn't think there would be. Mr. Donald loved his store just as it was, even though he would tell everyone about his yearly improvements. Everything in the store was the same except for some new frozen food cases on the left-hand side. Mr. Donald also added two round tables and chairs on each side of the old espresso maker, which his uncle Luigi sent him from Italy. It had been passed down through the generations, and he was proud to have it in his store. The floor was wooden and spotless. Mr. Donald mopped it every day after closing, and, once a month, waxed and buffed it.

What a lovely adventure it was to come to this grocery store with Gram when I was young. We would get a grocery cart that usually had a squeaky wheel and make our way through the produce aisle on the right side of the store. Mr. Donald had all the fruits and vegetables in bushel baskets, and Gram sniffed and squeezed to her heart's content. We would go up and down the aisles gathering the non perishables we needed, then to the refrigerated section for some dairy products and frozen goods. The last stop would be the butcher case that ran along the entire wall in the back of the store. It was filled with a variety of fresh cut meats. Mr. Donald would greet the customers and announce the specials of the day. I remember after Gram made her selection, Mr. Donald weighed it on a large scale that sat in the middle of the meat counter. Then he would wrap the meat in white butcher paper, seal it with some tan tape, and mark the price on it with a black wax crayon.

The old cash register sat on the checkout counter right before the exit door. When I was a little girl, I would hold my hands over my ears when Mr. Donald rang up our order because the solid brass register would finish its task with a loud dinging sound. After Gram received her change and her S&H Green Stamps, I would usually get a dime to slide into the soda machine, or a nickel for a candy bar.

Mr. Donald left me briefly to ring up some groceries for a customer. It was Mrs. Garzio. A woman in her eighties, she was a school teacher all of her life in Hopewell. After her husband died, Gram told me that Mrs. Garzio became very ill, and fell on some tough times financially. When she was sick, Gram would take meals to her, and Mr. Donald would send her a basket of groceries once a week until she recovered. As I watched him ring up her items, I saw that he only rang up every other one. Since her vision was not the best, she always made the comment that she got a lot for her money at his store, and she did not understand all the talk about the high food prices. Mr. Donald just smiled and agreed with her. Placing the groceries in her cart, she wheeled them out the door and around the corner where she lived. Mr. Donald winked at me as she left, and continued to prepare the coffee.

"How about a cinnamon roll, Tess?" he asked. "They are not as good as your Grams, but they are fresh."

"That sounds great, Mr. Donald."

"Come, come, Tess, sit down, and we can visit before the Saturday rush starts," he said, as he pointed to the table by the window. "So how have you been?" Mr. Donald asked.

"Oh, I've been quite busy and missing Gram an awful lot." I replied. "Since I've been back, I have been going through the house and the out buildings and trying to get all of Gram's things in order for the realtor and the auctioneer. I guess I never realized how much I missed it here," I said. "I never thought much about Hopewell since I moved to Boston, except when I came back to visit Gram. Even then the visit was short. I had so much on my mind with my job and my next assignment, that I didn't pay much attention to anything else. My stay here this time is different. I drift in and out of the past while I am staying here. Don't get me wrong, Mr. Donald, I do not want to live in the past, it just feels good to be connected to that part of me that is also timeless and more personal. I feel that way at Grams. I feel that way in Hopewell. I don't feel that way in Boston, and to tell you the truth, this is the first time I have admitted that to anyone. I'm beginning to find it difficult to think of the farm in the hands of a new owner. Do you think I am just being sentimental, Mr. Donald?"

He took a sip of the hot espresso that he had just poured into our cups.

"I think, Tess, when you do not feel like you need to find something, you don't look for it. When you do feel that you must find something, other than what you have, you get an urge to start searching for that something, and you do not stop until you find it," he said. "Perhaps you are beginning to look at life differently. Up to this point, I guess it was your success and fame that made you happy, but happiness may be presenting itself in a different way to you now. Maybe you reached a time in your life when you are searching for something else, and possibly coming back to your Gram's farm made you realize this."

"Mr. Donald, what if you find what you are looking for, but you are not sure you want it? Then what do you do?" I questioned.

"Well, Tess," he said, "maybe the uncertainty is not within you. Sometimes it's other people or events around us which may work against us, without meaning to, and prevent us from getting what we want. I'm not an expert at all this, Tess, but I've lived long enough to know that if you feel something different while you are here, you should at least give it some thought. It may mean taking some chances, but it is your life that you are talking about, so the chances are worth taking. If you don't follow what is in your heart and your soul, and you take the wrong turn, you may regret it the rest of your life. Who wants to look back on their years and wonder why?"

"I don't understand some of the things that are happening to me now? I think it is just being silly and overemotional. If I wanted to stay on the farm and live in Hopewell, I could have done it years ago. I chose a better life for myself, and that life is what I will return to next week."

Mr. Donald sat back in his chair, looked down at the parody as he rolled it between his fingers.

Then he looked up at me, placed it back in his mouth, and smiled.

"Sometimes, Tess, we make the right decision after trying all the wrong ones," he said. "That may take awhile." He took a bite of his cinnamon roll, a swig of coffee and headed to the counter to check out a customer. I finished my espresso and cinnamon roll and pulled Grams recipes out of my purse. I decided to make her ravioli and homemade sauce for dinner with Luke. After gathering all the ingredients, I made my way to the counter where Mr. Donald was talking with an elderly gentleman. He bagged his groceries, and walked around the counter to hand him the bag. He put his arm around the man's shoulder, as if he were wishing him well. Then he held the door open for him.

"That's Mr. Marcus. He just turned ninety," he said. His wife passed away last month. They were married sixty-five years, and he is having a hard time letting her go. Last week, I gave him a balloon, and I asked him to take it to the cemetery. I told him to stand in front of her grave and let the balloon go, and along with the balloon, his grief. I asked him to watch it rise until he did not see it anymore, and then picture it with his wife in that Special Place where she will be waiting for him when his time comes to go with her. He stopped in today to thank me and to let me know that he did as I suggested, and it helped him a lot."

Then Mr. Donald looked down at my order on the counter.

"Well, what do we have here, Tess?"

"I'm having Luke LeFevre, Jake's veterinarian, over for dinner tonight." I said. Mr. Donald raised his eyebrow.

"Luke LeFevre, I know him well. He stops in here once a week for groceries, and fills his cart with mostly frozen dinners and snacks. How did he manage to get himself invited for a home-cooked meal?"

I told Mr. Donald the story about Jake and our chance meeting with him in Herron, and the kindness he showed to us.

"I wanted to thank him for buying us dinner at the Herron diner, so I invited him over for supper," I said. "I'm going to make one of Gram's favorite pasta dishes."

"Just wait here for a minute, Tess."

Mr. Donald walked back to the meat case and returned with four sweet sausage patties.

"This is my gift for your dinner tonight. I always see Luke eyeing up this sausage, and when I ask him if he wants some, he always tells me that he doesn't know how to make it. He will be surprised."

He handed me a fresh loaf of Italian bread that was sitting in the case by the door.

"This is on the house too," he said.

"Well, thank you, Mr. Donald, you are so generous," I said.

He bagged my order, and since there was no one in line behind me, he motioned for me to go back over to the table.

"Do you want one more cup of espresso, Tess? Please, I don't know when I will be seeing you again," he said.

I agreed and sat down.

"I will tell Mrs. Bingenzo, I saw you," he said.

"Oh yes, Mr. Donald, please tell your lovely wife, Eva, that I said hello," I replied with some embarrassment at not thinking of that myself.

"You know, Tess, we just celebrated our anniversary. We are together fifty years. Now there is an example of what I was talking about before. If I made the wrong decision, I would have regretted it to this day," he said.

"What do you mean, Mr. Donald?" I asked.

"I met Eva when we were in high school, and we became high-school sweethearts. When it was time for me to leave for the Army after I graduated, I broke up with her because I thought that I would find excitement, adventure and romance in Europe where I was going to be stationed, and I did," he said grinning. "I met a girl in France, and, after a short time, we became engaged. I thought that she was the only girl for me because, you see, I let other things make that choice for me. I was a young American soldier with a big ego. I was in a romantic European country with a beautiful woman at my side. We stopped and had dinner at charming, sidewalk cafes. Everything around me was saying, 'this is for you, Don, this is the life you want,' he said shaking his head. "The strange thing was that even though I thought I had what I wanted, I missed Eva. I didn't write or phone her, but not a week went by since I last saw her that I did not think about her. Not a week, and that is the truth. Thank God I finally realized that she was the love of my life, and I broke off my engagement. When I got home, I called Eva hoping that she was not married. I was very fortunate to find out that she missed me too. Although she had a boyfriend, she was not eager to walk into the future with him. I guess you can say we were meant for each other, but see what could have happened if I didn't listen to my heart and soul, and made my decision based on other things."

"Did you ever regret your decision?" I asked "Not one day in fifty years have I regretted my decision," Mr. Donald said, shaking his folded hands in the air. "I cannot imagine my life without her."

He got up to direct a customer to an item. Then he returned to me.

"I don't know what made me tell you this today except, for some reason, I felt as if you were supposed to hear it from me. Speaking of Eva, look what your Gram made us for our anniversary."

Mr. Donald pointed to a beautifully framed needle point that was hanging on the wall. It was next to a picture of Eva and him that was taken on the day they got engaged. I looked at the wall, then I stared at what I read.

Dear Eva and Donald,
Happy Anniversary
The world is full wonder, each time a new sun breaks
And it leaves us with a story, as the moon and owl awake
The story is a message, for the open heart to take
The world is full wonder, each time a new sun breaks

"Tess, are you okay?" Mr. Donald asked.

"Yes, I am. I am more than okay. Thanks for the espresso, the talk, the delicious roll, and the food for dinner," I said.

Then I gave Mr. Donald a kiss on the cheek. Looking up at the framed words, one more time, I said to him,

"You have helped me more than you know."

As I left the store, I wasn't sure whether my words were meant for Mr. Donald or Gram.

Supper

I hurried home with the groceries, and started making the homemade tomato sauce. Trying to follow Gram's 'a little of this' and a 'handful of that' recipe, I finally got it all combined in the slow cooker. I put a chocolate cake in the oven and made a pot of Mr. Donald's espresso. It seemed strange, but I found myself standing in Gram's kitchen taking in the smells of marinara and cheese, olive oil and basil, garlic and onion, and chocolate and Italian coffee. For some unknown reason, I felt especially grateful. I chose Gram's off white lace tablecloth, beige cloth napkins, good china, and fine silverware when setting the table.

"What am I fussing about, Jake? It's just your vet coming to a home cooked dinner. Mr. Donald says he eats frozen dinners all the time anyway, so I don't think I have to fuss much," I said, looking at Jake but continuing to put some finishing touches to the table.

The tinted crystal wine glasses complimented the pink and green flowered dishes, matching salad bowls, and coffee cups and saucers. I added a vase of fresh flowers, and a scented candle that I bought on my way home from the grocery store. The finished table looked just perfect. The pasta, tomato sauce, meatballs, and sausage were combined and in the oven baking. With the salads prepared and in the refrigerator, and icing already on the cake, I went upstairs to get dressed. I put on a black skirt and white blouse, and finished off the outfit with black leather low heeled shoes. I sat down at Gram's dresser to put on some make up.

"I'm 'putting on my face,' Gram," I joked, smiling into the mirror, and adding some color to my cheeks.

I stood up, returned the dresser seat under the dresser, and turned to go downstairs. One more look, I thought, just to make sure. Looking into the mirror, Gram's picture sitting on the dresser, caught my eye. Mysteriously coming from the picture, was the sound of an old raspy voice.

"You look beautiful, Tess."

Ignoring what I thought I heard, I went downstairs to finish the supper and wait for Luke.

At six thirty, just like clockwork, I heard the Silverado coming up the road. Jake started to bark.

"Quiet, Jake, it's only Luke. You knew he was coming," I scolded.

From the corner of the window, I watched him park, step out of the truck, and pause a few minutes. With some hesitation, he began to walk toward the door with a bottle of wine in his hand. I opened the door before he had a chance to knock.

"Hi Luke, it's good to see you. I thought maybe you were changing your mind when you stepped out of your truck," I said.

I was already prepared to explain why I was watching him from the window, but thankfully, he did not ask.

"Why no, I just got a little nervous. I haven't done this in a long time," he said.

Surprised how nervous I felt as well, I quickly said.

"Me too," and then followed up with, "well at least we know that much about each other."

He laughed as he made his way into the house. Jake ran right up to him, and after the pats on the head and belly rubs, Luke and I walked into the kitchen.

"Shall I open this bottle of wine?" he asked, pulling a corkscrew out of his jacket pocket. "I brought my own because I thought the last thing Angeline would own would be this little gadget."

"Good thinking, Luke, you are probably right with that assumption," I said.

He poured the red wine for us, and offered me the first glass. I invited him into the parlor to wait for supper. We both took a seat on the chairs on each side of the fireplace. The warm fire took the chill out of the room, and it added some coziness to the evening.

Then there was silence, an uncomfortable kind of silence. After that, we both started to speak at the same time. Next, there was a pause, than an apology to each other, with insisting that the other go first. I felt just like I did at my high school dance when I finally got introduced to the boy I liked. I remember that moment. After rehearsing in front of the mirror all week, I didn't know what to say to Tony when I finally came face to face with him.

Luke made an attempt at some conversation, but it seemed strained, and I began to feel uncomfortable. I was grateful when the oven timer went off, signaling that Gram's pasta dish was done.

"Excuse me Luke," I said, "I need to check on dinner." Hastily making my exit from the parlor into the kitchen, I reached for the button on the oven panel to cancel the timer. To my amazement, I found that even though the bell went off, the timer was still ticking away the last fifteen minutes left on the dial.

"Thanks Gram," I said to myself, looking up at the ceiling. "I don't know how you did it, but you saved me from a particularly tense moment. Help me Gram, please. I want to try and get through this dinner with Luke, and hopefully head back to my everyday life in my own home."

I turned off the oven, poured some more wine into my glass, and returned to the parlor.

"More wine Luke?" I asked.

"No, thank you, I think I will wait until dinner."

"I decided to call it supper, in honor of Gram," I said.

"What a coincidence," Luke said. "It's funny that you should mention that. Since I moved to Hopewell, I always refer to my last meal of the day as supper. I find it rather humbling."

"Well, if you are ready and hungry, I've made one of Gram's favorite dishes," as I waved my hand to usher him into the kitchen. "The sausage and the bread are courtesy of Mr. Donald. He wanted to know why I was buying all this food, and I explained to him that you were coming to dinner tonight. He thought you might enjoy the sausage and the bread. He said your specialty is frozen dinners and snacks."

133

"He gives all of my secrets away," Luke said smiling, "but I will thank him for his generosity when I see him." Luke sat down at the table, and I served dinner. The scent of the carnations, combined with the time honored Italian aroma in this traditional old kitchen, added to the simplicity of the evening.

"What a wonderful idea to put a sprig of rosemary in your napkins, Tess, Luke commented.

I looked down at the napkins, and sure enough, there was the rosemary. I did not remember putting it in the napkin for our dinner tonight, but I immediately thought of Gram's tradition for her special celebrations. Not knowing what to say, and hoping Luke didn't notice my surprise, I simply replied,

"Thank you, Luke."

All of a sudden, it felt comfortable and natural for me to be here, and for Luke to be here too. For some strange reason, the strained dialogue turned into easy conversation. What changed, I thought, walking from the parlor to the kitchen? What happened between the first glass of wine, and the first forkful of pasta? Then I remembered the oven timer going off early, and now, the rosemary. The answer was right in front of me. It was the veiled hand of Gram moving about in her kitchen, and helping me as she always did. Thank you Gram, I said to myself, as the flickering candle caught my attention, and the fragrance of Patchouli suddenly drifted toward me.

"Tess, a penny for thoughts," Luke said. "You look as if you are somewhere else."

"Oh Luke, I am sorry, but for some reason I began to think about Gram," I said. "I use to think that people didn't need the guidance of their Grams after they grew up, but in this moment, I've realized that it is just not true."

"Well, I wish to tell you again if you didn't hear me," he said, "that the food is delicious, and I want to thank you for taking the time to prepare this tasty supper for me. You are an excellent cook."

Tess smiled.

"Thank you, Luke, but the credit goes to Gram. Cooking pasta was an art to her, and the sauce, well, that creation is from her mother. She was extremely particular about her sauce."

"I can believe that, but you are the one who cooked the delicious food that I ate here tonight. With all due respect to Gram, I want to give the praise to you," Luke said.

We had dessert and espresso in the parlor while listening to a Frank Sinatra hour long serenade on Gram's radio. The song 'Where or When' began to play, and the words to that song probably spurred my next question to Luke.

"Luke, do believe spirits make visits back to us to help us along our way?" I asked.

"Interesting question, Tess, I need a swig of espresso before I answer that question," he said smiling. "Well, let's see, I'm sixty, and if there is anything I am sure of at my age," Luke said, "it is that I am unsure of everything. With that said, my first impulse is to answer your question with a resounding, yes."

He sat back in his chair and looked relaxed. He stretched out his legs and crossed one ankle over the other.

"I believe that our loved ones do come back to us, not in a physical body, but rather in their spirit form. Let me tell you why I say that. I am not at all a religious man, and I am not a practicing churchgoer, but I believe there is an immeasurable Power out there that I am incapable of comprehending with my own limited intelligence. I can't give it a name, but I know it is there, and I humbly respect It. I believe that it is so finely tuned that anything that happens in this universe, happens according to its impeccable timing, and its perfect and flawless consent. The mystery of the spirit intrigues me. I guess until we finally cross over, we can never truly know the magnitude of what the spirit can achieve. I cannot prove it, but I believe that my father's spirit was the inspiration that changed my life."

He took another bite of the chocolate cake, and another sip of the espresso. Then he continued.

135

"My father was a remarkable doctor and a truly humble man. I wish I could say that about myself. When I started out, I did not follow in his unassuming footsteps. I chose to do my internship at The Diamond Collar Clinic, an elite and expensive veterinary practice in Manhattan. Even when I made the switch to Hopewell, I still thought I was an upper class, high-steppin vet."

"Didn't you want to be a country vet and help animals in a small town?" I questioned.

"Yes, there was a part of me that wanted to do that, but realizing that I wanted to come to Hopewell, was only the beginning. I had some work to do on myself before I started to figure out some very valuable things that were part of my decision. I first needed to realize that I was not more sophisticated and intelligent because I came from New York City, studied at a prestigious university, and mingled with the rich and famous. In fact, the people in Hopewell were way ahead of me in that department," he paused and smiled. He continued. "After a few years and some hard knocks, I finally realized that I didn't choose this town, it chose me, and I didn't save these people, they saved me.

"Did your father teach you all this, Luke? I asked.

"I watched my father die a painful death from cancer, and that was when my lesson began. He told me that death was part of the deal we make when our spirit takes on the human body and comes into this world. He had unbelievable courage and faith that came from a much deeper place. He taught me how to die, and that is when I really learned how to live. Until the moment of his death, he was very aware of what was going on around him. It was in those moments that he started to teach me, and, I swear, he continued through his spirit after he died. I was there when he said his last good-bye, and he reminded me to listen to the voices around me, and listen very carefully. It took a while before I was convinced that what he told me was true.

Anyway, as the years past, I finally, began to pay attention to those voices, and through them came my father's guidance. I learned to stay open to that Power I told you about, and I cannot say enough about what it has sent back to me. Some days it comes through my patients, other days through people that I unexpectedly meet. Many times, I hear it in the quiet hours of the evening when I sit in my easy chair in front of the fireplace. Oh! it's my father's voice all right, and he knows exactly what I need. One of the first things that he helped me with was responsibility. I began to understand that the responsibility for me rests with me, not only for the good I did, but also for the bad, for I created both with the decisions I made. That was a hard lesson to learn, and I'm glad my father didn't give up on me.

Another tough lesson was learning to temper my ego. He taught me to put it aside when it got in my way. I swear my father's spirit persisted until I no longer clung to that ego. Then I discovered what real power was all about. So, Tess, I look for the signs and listen very consciously for the voice. Maybe unconsciously is a better word for it. An unexpected phone call, an unanticipated conversation with a friend, an event in our lives can move us in a different direction."

"So you're happy where you are in life, Luke?" I asked.

"Don't get me wrong, Tess, I have a long way to go. Falling is the natural process in learning how to walk. Every day, I try to be a better man. I am grateful to be alive and I am actually beginning to understand myself, and respect who I am becoming. My father's voice does not come around as often anymore, so I suppose that I am on the right track. Still, when I question an outcome, when decisions get difficult, or when I am full of doubt, I know he is hovering over me. Somehow, my thoughts are led to the peace and strength he showed all of his life, especially in his dying hour. I may have to listen to his words a little closer, but eventually all my questions receive answers, and all my doubts usually disappear.

I sat there amazed at what he was telling me. Maybe all the mysterious things that were happening to me were not mysterious after all. Maybe they were an attempt by my Gram to reach across from where she was and knock on the

137

door of my heart and soul. Perhaps this is a beginning for me. I took a deep breath, and a sip of my now cold coffee. I chose not to share my thoughts with Luke, not tonight anyway. I still had doubts. I had many doubts however Mr. Donald finally convinced me that those uncertainties may mean that new possibilities were at hand. I remembered his words, 'if you feel something different while you are here, you should at least give it some thought.'

"Luke, that is so inspiring," I continued. "Thank you so much, for sharing that with me. I loved hearing every minute of it. I do believe in a Power greater then myself. I believe that we are not alone in this world. I believe in the spirit, and I believe in the mystery of it all."

"There is a lot to learn," Luke said, "and we could never possibly cover it all tonight. It's ten already, and I need to get going. Are we still on for the Spring Fest parade in Herron tomorrow?" he asked.

"I was hoping we could still go," I answered.

"I will pick you up around eight tomorrow morning, if that is okay with you. It takes about three hours to get to Herron, and we should try to be there a little earlier if we want to set up our chairs by the judge's table. That is a good spot because the groups usually give their best performance in front of the judges."

"Okay, I will be ready," I said.

We walked to the door, and Luke turned to face me.

"Thanks for one of the best evenings I have had in a long time, Tess" he said. "Everything was perfect. The food was delicious, and you are a beautiful lady. I will see you tomorrow. Good night to you."

"Thank you for all your kind words." I said. "Good night, Luke, and I look forward to seeing you tomorrow."

Giving Jake a pat on his head, Luke swung the screen door open, and it squeaked as it closed behind him. I watched his truck disappear down the dirt road, then I headed to the kitchen to clean up. After putting everything away where it belonged, I turned off the lights. I started to head upstairs when I noticed that I forgot to blow out the Patchouli candle that was still burning on the kitchen table. As I walked toward it, the flame started to wildly dance and flicker. I stared at it and smiled. Then as crazy as it seemed, I responded as if I were answering a question.

"Yes, Gram, the evening has gone remarkably well, and yes, I am looking forward to seeing Luke tomorrow," I said out loud. "I guess you are quite proud of yourself for pulling this all together. Well, maybe it was you, or maybe it wasn't, but my plans have not changed. I will find suitable people to buy this farm, and I will be returning to Boston next week."

I took two more steps toward the table, and just as I was about to douse the flame, it mysteriously went out on its own. I smiled and shook my head.

"Good night, Gram," I said. "Don't be upset with me. I love you so much."

Day Nine

I left Jake sleeping and minding the house for the day, and I went outside to wait for Luke. He arrived promptly at eight.

"Good morning to you Tess," he said with a big smile on his face.

"Good morning to you, Luke," I said smiling back.

He helped me into the truck, made sure he had the canvas chairs in the back, and climbed into the driver's seat. I could smell the aroma of fresh diner coffee coming from the two cups that sat in holders in the middle console.

"It should be a beautiful day," Luke said. "It's a little chilly, but the people of Herron say that after they celebrate the Spring Fest, the weather turns warmer. I'm not convinced it's the magic they perform during the festival, as much as it may be Mother Nature moving us closer to March 21."

Luke looked almost the same as he did when I first met him, minus the fishing hat and the waders. He wore his Herron tackle shop shirt and blue jeans, and a light weight olive green jacket with a red cardinal sewn on the front pocket.

"Do you like cardinals?" I asked Luke. "The cardinal is my favorite bird. They look so majestic eating at the feeders, or sitting on a bare branch. Their vibrant red color really stands out against the winter snow. Yes, Tess, I am partial to that particular fine feathered friend, and I hope that I could return as one someday.

The conversation on our drive up was simple and enjoyable. Luke talked about his patients, and I chatted about my upcoming projects. We sipped our coffee and enjoyed the scenery of the bare hillsides being nudged out of their deep winter sleep. We arrived in Herron and parked at the diner.

"Breakfast first," Luke said.

We sat down in the same booth that we shared for supper a few days earlier. Before we knew it, our order was taken and our food served. Luke paid the check, and we were back in the truck and looking for an empty curb space to park. We got lucky, and found one next to the old hotel.

"This is a favorite place of mine," he said, pointing to the long-standing building. "This is where I stay when I come to Herron for two weeks of peace and quiet and spring fishing. I enjoy the ambiance here. It reminds me of the old days when a traveler would enter the hotel, walk up to a simple check-in desk, and ask for a room. After the clerk checked the guest ledger, he would return with a key that he retrieved from a slotted wooden box hanging on the wall that contains other room keys. The halls in this hotel are long and drab with just enough light to guide the visitor to his room that is hidden behind one of many mahogany doors. The transoms above the doors allow for some air flow and the transfer of muffled chatter from other guests as they make their way down the hall to their rooms. It soothes me to sleep," he said, taking a deep breath. "There are no phones in the rooms. Messages are left and picked up at the desk. There are no televisions either except for the one in the tavern where people gather in the evening. Fishing stories and the news of the town are discussed. People relax in comfortable leather chairs in front of the stone fireplace, or at the bar where the travelers are refreshed. All in all, it is a setting from the past that I look forward to reliving every year."

Luke helped me out of the truck, grabbed the chairs, and we found a spot not too far from the judges stand.

"This will be a great place to see the groups perform," he said.

Yes, I thought, it looked just the as it did when I came here as a child. It was the usual scene that appears just before a small town parade begins. The children are all excited and waiting for the parade to start. The vendors dress in their flat straw hats, red and white striped shirts, and black suspenders that hold up their black, baggy pants. They are pushing their carts in front of them filled with popcorn, candy, soda, and other goodies. A variety of stuffed animals hang from each side, and balloons, attached to the handle, toss and turn in the air. The clowns roam the streets doing tricks and giving away candy.

The siren sounded, ending my reminiscing and initiating the celebration of the spring planting, the summer cultivation, and the reaping of the fall harvest. The Herron Men's choir sang the National Anthem over the loudspeaker, and the parade began.

I looked at Luke and smiled. He responded by reaching for my hand and giving it a quick squeeze. It felt so comfortable to have such a good friend. I was surprised that I felt this way since I had just met him a few days ago, and it usually took me much longer before I would call anyone a dear friend.

The first cars passed us as the entourage of Herron officials presented themselves to the crowd. As the model T drove by, its occupant, dressed in an old fashioned suit and a top hat, looked directly at us and waved.

"Hello Luke, good to see you," he said, quickly. Luke waved back.

"Who was that?" I asked. "Oh, just the mayor," Luke chuckled.

"You know the mayor of Herron too?" I questioned.

"Yea, his Bulldog is my patient. He drives down to my office whenever Champ needs some care. The mayor is a good guy. Herron is lucky to have him as their leader," Luke said.

The fire engines passed by next and threw out candy to the kids. The Herron firefighters were all dressed in their fire proof coats and helmets and were standing next to the ladders in the back of the trucks. The high-school bands came next.

As they waved their flags and started to perform, my thoughts took me back to this familiar place when I was growing up. The memory was bittersweet. The connection to the past was strong today, and for some reason, I felt that Luke had something to do with that strong of connection.

I vividly remember Gram and Gramps sitting in the front seat of their car as we drove to the parade every March. They enjoyed their coffee and talked while I sipped chocolate milk and ate Gram's chocolate chip cookies from a paper bag in the back seat. I smiled at the thought of getting so excited and surprised at seeing the same event every year. How innocent childhood can be, I thought, when there is no need to make sense of the complicated world, rather just connect with the simple, the ordinary, the unspectacular.

I remember sitting on the curb with my elbows resting on my knees, and my hands cupping my face. I would fantasize about what I wanted to be when I grew up. Then suddenly, I would become whoever was performing in front of me. One minute, I became the bandleader. I was dressed in a white and blue double breasted, silver buttoned suit, and an impressive feathered headdress. Marching backwards, I would move my silver baton to the tempo of the music, as the musicians gave an outstanding performance to the crowd. The next minute, I became Miss Herron, sitting on a beautifully decorated float. I was the pretty girl dressed in her elegant, ruby gown and dazzling, rhinestone crown waving to the crowd. Then I turned into a proud member of a prestigious Armed Services division. Perhaps an officer wearing the distinguished uniform of a veteran, who carried the stately appearance of devotion, the enduring courage of battle, as well as, the irreplaceable expression of tragic loss. It was hard to believe that over a half century of my days had already passed, and I pursued a profession other than what I had imagined. Today I was not sure that I was where I should be. Where did the time go? I smelled the festival in the air and felt the small town in my bones. I felt connected to everyone and everything, and for a split second, I felt the urge to change my direction in mid stream and come back to it all. I always believed that the pursuit of my own happiness was the most important thing, and I still felt that way, but oddly enough, what I was experiencing at this moment was a passion to move beyond where my life had already taken me. I felt an overwhelming, peculiar desire to finish the race running on well known country roads, and not rushing down unfamiliar streets in distant cities.

My thoughts were abruptly disturbed when I heard Luke call my name.

"Tess, did you like the bagpipes? It's a new group from up the line. Rumor has it that they were very good. I'm glad we heard them perform," Luke said.

"Yes, Luke, they were excellent," I replied even though I wasn't sure I heard their music at all.

For some strange reason, they were drowned out by a somewhat familiar voice from the past that was stronger and louder than the bagpipes. She was speaking of sweet regret along with the hope of a new day. Her resounding words were now in the beats of my heart, and the depths of my soul. There she was speaking to me through a simple parade, in an unpretentious town, with a down-to-earth man at my side.

The parade ended, and Luke and I walked around the community park to see what the vendors had to offer. We ordered some grilled bison burgers and fresh cut French fries. We sampled some caramel corn, and homemade ice cream. The day had been just wonderful. It was about two in the afternoon when we drove down Main Street. Luke slowly turned left at the intersection, and we headed back to Hopewell.

At the farm, Luke parked the Silverado near the barn and helped me out of the truck. Jake was barking and probably imagining that some stranger was invading his territory. I opened the door, and he ran circles around us. He was displaying in his doggie behavior that he was overjoyed to see us and wanted to play. Luke reached into his pocket and pulled out a treat. Jake took it from him and ran behind the barn to eat it.

"Do you always carry dog snacks in your pocket, Luke?" I said laughing.

"It's my job to make sure all the animals I know are cared for and rewarded," he said smiling.

The moment seemed awkward. Luke declined the invitation to come in and visit for a while, saying that he still needed to stop and check on the colt and mare, then get ready for an early Monday morning at the clinic.

"Thanks for a great couple of days, Tess," he said. "I'm glad we met. I could have never planned something like this, even if I tried. I guess it's true. We never know what lies ahead for us."

Again, I saw the gentle look on his face supported by his unwavering confidence.

"It has been great, Luke, and I thank you for everything. I will be at the clinic Tuesday for Jake's check up, and to say good bye. Maybe you can visit Boston some time, and I can show you around the city," I replied.

"Well, thank you, Tess, maybe I will take you up on that sometime. Things have worked out so well this time though without our planning, maybe we should allow fate to determine our next meeting too."

He leaned over and gave me a light kiss on my check.

"For now though, I just feel so amazingly lucky to have met someone, who I find it so difficult to say good bye to." With that, he gave Jake another treat and a pat on the head. He turned around, jumped into his truck, and waved good bye. Then he slowly headed down the dirt road.

As I watched Luke drive away, I was glad my stay here was almost over. Being at Grams, seeing people from my past, meeting Luke, and seeing the parade were all good, but at the same time, it was causing some confusion in my life. Today was a perfect way to end my stay here. Next week, I thought, I will tie up all the loose ends, bundle up all the memories, and head back to Boston with Jake.

It was early evening and the sky was preparing for the night. The air was crisp and cool with some cloud cover. There was a hint of rain in the air. Gram would have loved a night like this, I thought.

All at once, Jake started to bark. He rushed back and forth behind the barn, and looked confused. He stopped, tilted his head, raised his tail, and took off up the hill into to the woods, as if he were chasing something or responding to a call.

"Jake, come here," I called. "Jake, come to me, boy."
He paid no attention to my call and continued running.

"Jake," I shouted again, but he continued to move up the hill. I started to run after him. I hurried up the path that led behind the barn, and followed him into the woods. I could hardly keep up with him. This was so unlike Jake. He rarely took off like this, and when he did, he would turn around and come back when Gram or I called to him.

"Jake, Jake, come back," I yelled, but he just kept running. Through the trees and bushes, I saw he was heading in the direction of the Springhouse. I followed him down the path that led to the Springhouse, pushing aside the bare branches until I came to the clearing where the Springhouse stood. Jake was sitting next to Gram's bench. He turned around and looked at me, but seemed very uneasy.

"Jake, what are you doing?" I reprimanded. "Where are you going? Come on boy, let's get back to the house before it gets dark."
I turned around to head back, but Jake did not follow. Rather, he was up on all fours and circling Gram's bench. He began to sniff and whimper.

"Oh, I understand now. You miss Gram."
I turned and walked toward him.

"Well, so do I, Jake. I miss her a lot," I said, as my voice started to crack, and tears filled my eyes.

"Now, come on, let's go," I commanded.
Jake just looked up at me, and then started to dig feverishly on the side of the bench where Gram usually sat.

"Now, what are you doing?" I questioned.
Still paying no attention to me, he continued to dig and pull at something buried in the dirt.

"What is it boy? What do you have there?" I asked. Kneeling down, I pulled something out of the hole that he dug.

The Path

It was a small black plastic bag tightened with a rubber band and a sprig of rosemary. Around the rubber band was a gold ribbon, and attached to the gold ribbon was one of Gram's homemade dog bones that Jake always loved.

"Oh I see what you were after, Jake, but how did you smell this all the way down by the barn? Well, come on over here, and enjoy it. I think Gram put it here especially for you. If you were smart enough to find it, than you deserve to eat it."

I sat down on Gram's bench, and began to unravel the ribbon and release the treat. Jake took it gently from my hand and laid down to enjoy it. As I was about to roll up the plastic, and put it in my pocket, I noticed a piece of paper sticking out of the bag. It looked as if it had Gram's handwriting on it. With enough of the evening light left, I started to read.

Dear Tess
I was hoping that you and Jake would find your way to the Springhouse. It was such a special place for us to sit together and enjoy the moment. Remember when we would snack on some delicious cherries that we picked, and then put the rest in the Springhouse to stay fresh. Before I became ill, I put a jar in there for you. It sits on the shelf above the cool running water.
Gram

I raised my eyes from the letter that was now trembling in my hand, and stared straight ahead at the old stone spring house door...

Gram at the Springhouse

Gram's Bench

The Springhouse was built in 1840 to shelter the water that poured from the free-flowing springs in the hillsides. Made from field stone, it was about eight feet by ten feet with one door and one window. The spring water came in through a trough laid in a tunnel. Set into the hillside the way it was, the temperature remained almost constant, winter and summer.

The tunnel through which the spring water came was constructed with stone walls laid up like the rest of the spring house, and then covered with more hand cut stones made into an arched roof which extended about twenty feet, or more, into the hillside. Above the tunnel was a French drain to support the wall, set into the hillside. In the Springhouse there was a cistern. When this was full of water, it overflowed into the trough which was made from a solid block of stone. At one point, our kitchen had running water that came directly from this underground spring.

Slowly, I walked toward the Springhouse. I moved down the two stone steps, and disengaged the lock with the key that hung above it on the door frame. As I nudged the door open, a damp odor eased out. In an instant, my sense of smell rolled back time.

I looked up toward the thick wooden ledge above the flowing water. There, as she promised, was a full jar of cherries. Alongside of it was another jar, and inside that jar was a piece of paper. Reaching for both, I sat down on the stone ledge of the cistern. It was dark inside the Springhouse. I searched for the small emergency flashlight that I always kept in my coat pocket, and snapping it on, I placed it on my lap while I twisted the lid off the jar.

"My God, it's a letter from Gram," I said out loud. Why would she leave me a letter that's sealed in a jar in the Springhouse? What would have made her do that? I may never have found it here, I thought. I held the light closer to the page, and I began to read the words. All of a sudden, they were being read to me, and the raspy voice I heard was Grams.

My dearest Tess,

Do not weep for me, for I will always be with you, and we shall see each other again someday. My journey on this earth has almost ended, and I am getting ready to be called back to my true Home. I have lived for many years and have enjoyed this beautiful earth, but now I am about to lay down for a short time and take a nap. Please do not think that the doctors could have done more to prolong my life, for let me assure you, Tess, the Voice that is calling me back Home is infallible and has, and will always have, impeccable timing.

As the time nears, I become less and less afraid of the physical ending. I realize that my body will alter, but I know that the Life of my spirit will live forever. This almighty Life that moves the waves of the oceans and lifts the wings of the birds will, without a doubt, lead me in its direction and path.

I have left this letter for you in the Springhouse for several reasons, Tess. I would be remiss if I did not share with you the beautiful gift about life that I have come to know in my years on this earth. With open arms, I invite you to the place where I received it. Right here, at this humble Springhouse, I have learned to discover myself from the inward spirit to the outward appearance.

You have done well, Tess. Through an education, you have pursued a distinguished career that has led you into a prosperous and comfortable lifestyle, and there is nothing wrong with that. You have become extremely successful in many respects however those things are human achievements, necessary to support and live. They are not spiritual ones, necessary to grow and live on. Sometimes, we may forget that we need both. We become so absorbed in our human perspective that we tend to overlook the spirit which is powerful and beyond measure. Always aware of our higher good, it constantly tries to remind us of the real reason we came to live on this earth. The Voice is difficult to hear in this noisy world, but it never stops looking for opportunities to be heard. I am confident that eventually it will capture your attention and urge you in its direction. The water you see in front of you, finds its own level by flowing around, through, above, and below the barriers in its path. Its force can smooth out rough edges. A river can cut through stone with its cleansing and restoring strength, it only takes time.

My life has been filled with many twists and turns, and I still struggle to bend my mind around all of them. I think we usually have to stray a bit before we stumble upon the true reason why we are here. I guess we are not meant to settle down to early in our lives.

When I was young, before you and I came to know each other, I didn't always believe as I do now. Yes, I was brought up to believe that there was a God 'out there' that watches over us, and sometimes intervenes for us. I was taught to do good deeds, and I did, but always seeking the recognition and praise in return. I measured my worth and gauged my appeal on the opinions of the people around me. You see, Tess, I didn't have to live in a big city to become self centered. Even in the little town of Hopewell, it was an easy feat to accomplish. Self interest isn't a place you travel to on the outside. It is a place you make your way to within. The vehicle that usually takes us there are the things our insensitive eyes refuse to see. I muted the voices that wanted to help me out, until I could no longer ignore them.

Then, somewhere along the way, I was given a gift. As sure as the night follows the day, the Giver of the gift was knocking on the door of my heart and soul, on my bench at the Springhouse. Simple as it may seem, I just needed to be quiet in order to hear it, and then it all began.

In the beginning, I started going to the Springhouse in the early morning just to drink my coffee and get some fresh air before I started my chores on the farm. I didn't go there to pray, or for that matter, think about God. Then I began to come back in the late evening, for no other reason than to get away from the family and relax. I started to enjoy the quiet here, and it was in that quiet that I started to think about things differently. It took a while, but I amazingly began to gain interest in those thoughts. It's incredible what you hear when you are still. As time went on, I began to figure out that by listening to this Voice within me, a Voice of which I was not the source, I was being guided in another direction in my life. Before I knew it, I started to live that direction, and it felt good. Imagine that, Tess, I was connecting with something greater than myself at this humble Springhouse. That is when I came to believe in my Spirit. This Spirit that completed me encompassed everything that was around me. Once you have heard the voice of your soul, and make the journey in your heart and your mind, there is no going back. Once you have found your true direction, it is difficult not to follow it. Prayer simply became talking to a greater Intellect, and the answers came back to me in some purely simple forms. I heard it through a rumbling thunder in the distance, a deer walking through the woods, the unassuming chirping of a cricket, the retiring call of a cardinal, or the peaceful sound of the fresh water running from the mountain spring. As time went on, I looked forward to coming to the Spring-house every day because there I could stop the motion, find a niche to listen, and embrace a Presence that filled me with energy and enthusiasm for life. It was not so much a way of thinking, but more so a way of being that didn't include self importance or external applause. For this magnificent change, my Guide deserved my deepest and humblest respect.

So Tess, along with the tangible gifts of the house and the farm, I leave with you some intangible gifts that were given to me at this Springhouse.

The Gift of Silence

I learned to be quiet. Through it, I received unexpected answers to questions, profound guidance, freedom from binding habits, and to accept things just as they are. I began to understand that silence brings wisdom, and wisdom brings answers to our prayers. There are many ways to pray, and taking a deep breath is just one of them.

The Gift of Forgiveness
I learned to say I'm sorry. When I began to forgive myself and others, I was set free from the self of yesterday. I realized that the relationship that matters the most is the one that I have with myself, and I was in charge of it. If slipped up or let myself down, I could start again, at any given moment, to be a better person.

The Gift to Love
I learned to say I love you. By giving openly to the people around me and not expecting anything in return, I came to realize perfect love. After a while, I began to pay it forward.

The Gift of Life
I learned to appreciate the moment. With this gift, I began to live every moment to its fullest, so that when the last days of my life were upon me, I walked away from the table satisfied and without saying a word.

The Gift of Simplicity
I learned that I didn't need many things to make me happy. Life became effortless, natural, and ordinary.

The Gift of Gratitude
I learned to say thank you. By thanking God many times throughout the day for everything I received, I realized how much I was actually given. The more grateful I became, the more I found to be grateful for.

From that time on, Tess, with these gifts in hand, my life took on a new meaning. I have tried to keep this farm because I could not imagine myself living anywhere else but here. I have left this farm to you because I cannot picture you living anywhere else either. There is a certain peace about this land and house that I have come to know and love. If you choose not to stay, the gifts I received here can be yours anywhere, you only need to open your heart and your soul to them. The choice is yours and yours alone although therein lies the challenge. To find happiness and peace, sometimes you must be willing to give up what you have for what you want even more. That can bring with it some struggle, uncertainty, and even difficulty in letting go of your past life, but they are just growing pains of a new self. Eventually, you will move past them and toward the calm assurance that enables you to be thankful for even those growing pains.

There is a wind behind each of us, Tess, and if we allow it to guide us, in time, it will take us to where we are supposed to go. Preparing for that moment can take a lifetime. Remember, a young child responds freshly to every instant, you can too.

With all that I have told you, Tess, you can understand why I have asked you to spread some of my ashes at the Springhouse. This is where the gifts were offered to me, and this is where I finally chose to embrace them. Whether you stay or whether you go, I want to leave a part of me here.

Be well, Tess,
My Love to you,
Gram

Except for the dim circle of light coming from the flashlight, it was dark and cold in the Springhouse. The jar of cherries sat next to me, and I held her letter in my hand. With tears in my eyes, I looked out the open door toward Grams bench. It appeared stark and abandoned in the night. In all my years, and with all my education, I had not learned the word that could explain how I felt at this moment.

"Please Gram do not leave me to make such a choice by myself. Please Gram," I prayed.

I listened closely for a response, but there was nothing but silence. I closed my eyes and waited, but there was nothing. **Then she was in front of me.**

I rubbed my eyes in disbelief, but the apparition did not disappear. As clear as day, Gram was sitting on her bench just like she use to.

"Come, keep me company, Tess. Have some cherries." I heard her say as she patted her hand on the bench next to her. Jake began to bark and ran to the bench. I walked outside of the Springhouse and toward the image. Reluctantly, I sat down next to her.

"Remember when we would sit here and read stories, and laugh out loud," she continued. "Remember when we would dance around the trees and pretend we were falling leaves?" I nodded my head slowly.

"Come, Tess, take my hand and let's dance again just like we use to," she said.

She got up and extended her hand to me. Taking it, I felt nothing. We began to whirl around, waltzing to the music. Hundreds of stars lit up the sky. Jake pranced around after us. She led and I followed, and when I finally gazed into her eyes, those eyes that I will never forget, I suddenly realized what Gram meant. I felt as if I belonged here. As we danced wildly, her apron waved in the breeze as she turned around and around. With each turn we made, I began to feel stronger, and then wiser, and then humble, and finally willing.

In a blink of an eye, as quickly as she appeared, she was gone, and I found myself dancing alone. I looked around for her, and unable to find her anywhere, I sat down on her bench with my face hidden in my hands. I thought I was crying, but my eyes were dry. I remained there for what seemed like hours, but, in reality, were just minutes.

Then slowly raising my head, I sat posed and staring at the Springhouse. All at once, I felt like a butterfly emerging from its cocoon and leaving behind the guise of a caterpillar. I felt like a seed that evolves into a bud, then blooms into a beautiful flower.

I started to smile, then I started to smile some more, then I couldn't stop smiling. I knew, in those moments, it wasn't that I loved my life in Boston less, it was that I loved this farm and home more. I realized that I wasn't a perfect woman by any means, but with a little work in the right direction, I could become a person that my soul would be proud of. The gift at this Springhouse, wasn't that Gram had changed. The real gift at this Springhouse was that I had. Holding Gram's letter in one hand and the flashlight in the other, Jake and I made our way down the hill and back to the house. Like the circle of light ahead of me, her words led the way.

The world is full wonder, each time a new sun breaks
It leaves us with a story, as the moon and owl awake
The story is a message, for the open heart to take
The world is full wonder, each time a new sun breaks

Day Ten

When I woke up early the next day, my eyes moved about Grams room as I lay in her bed. I wondered if last night were just a dream although Jake's muddy paw prints on Gram's bedroom rug had suggested otherwise.

I was thankful I came to live with my Gram and Gramps. It's awfully strange where life leads us, and even stranger the reasons why, I thought. If my father had taken the train later that day, he would not have been in the accident. If he was not in that accident, my mom and I would have never moved to Gram's. If my mother did not get sick and die, I would not have been left in Grams care, and if I had never been left in Grams care, I would have missed this moment-in-time. Fate works in very strange ways, I thought.

Gram would call it the Divine Plan. She believed that everything happens for a reason, and what we believe to be a tragedy when it happens, may become our greatest gift for our highest good as we go through our years. Even though she left this earth, she has dared to reach across from the other side to encourage and inspire me. Gram believed in me more than I believed in myself.

"I don't know how you did it Gram," I said out loud, moving my head back and forth against the pillow. "I went into that Springhouse last night determined to leave all this behind, and I came out doubting my decision. I cannot promise anything, Gram, but I have a lot to think about."

With that thought, I got out of bed, grabbed some breakfast, and headed to the clinic with Jake. Luke was just getting out of his truck when I arrived.

"Good morning, Luke," I said, as Jake and I got out of the car.

"Good morning, Tess," Luke replied, with a puzzled look on his face. "What are you doing here so early?"

"I came to ask you for a favor, Luke. Do you think you can keep Jake for the day? I have some pressing business to take care of today, and I can't take him with me. Do you have some room for a border?" Tess asked.

"I sure do. I'll do better then that. He could sit in my office, and at lunch time I'll treat him to a hamburger. The clinic closes at five today. If you're not back by then, I'll take him home with me tonight, and you can pick him up tomorrow. It will give me time to do his checkup and spend time with him before he leaves," Luke said.

"Thanks, Luke," Tess replied.

"Take your time and have a good day, Tess. Come on Jake, let's get to work."

Luke unlocked the clinic door, waved goodbye, and he and Jake entered the building. Back in the car, I closed my eyes for a brief moment. I was glad Luke didn't ask questions.

"You better be right about all this, Gram," I said out loud as I started the car and drove north into Herron.

Grabbing a cup of coffee, and an egg sandwich at the Herron diner, I headed up to the top of the west rim of the canyon. On a bench, overlooking the canyon, I ate my breakfast. Again, I felt the need to call on Gram.

"Okay, Gram," I mumbled, "you have always been such an influence in my life. I hope, against all odds, that I was not just imagining what happened last night. You handed me some directions, but you forgot to give me a road map. Before I make a quick judgment or hasty decision, I need more guidance. This is my life we are talking about here. If I did not see it for myself, I would never believe all the strange things that have happened to me since I have been back. I lead a busy life, Gram. I do not have time for imaginings. There are a lot of people I love to be with, and things I love to be part of up in Boston. I find my life fascinating there. I want to know for sure if I am about to do the right thing. Please, Gram, this may be a defining moment in my life. I need one more sign, and I will not doubt my decision again. I promise you, Gram, just one more, and I will not look back or ask again."

I waited but nothing happened. Then I remembered what Mrs. Como told me about the signs along the way. 'Those valuable lessons come when we least expect them, Tess, all we can do is to keep our eyes and hearts open, and just hope we do not miss them. Yes, Tess, we must hope that we do not miss them.'

With no sign from Gram in sight, I walked back to the car. After searching through my purse for the keys and not being able to find them, I traced my steps back to the canyon vista, where I stood a few minutes ago. There on the bench, lay my car keys, and there on the iron railing perched a red-tailed hawk.

"Gram?" I whispered.

I looked around hoping that no one heard me call her name.

"Gram?" I said again.

With that, the hawk flew away, only to begin making wide circles in the sky above the canyon.

"Oh, Gram, it is you. I know it is. It was in your book. You wrote about the hawk."

I surprised myself that I remembered the verse.

We hear roar of the mighty river, the trickle of the stream flight of the soaring eagle, the gliding hawk on wing
Aware that the mighty spirit, inspires the human dream the roar of the mighty river, lifts the gliding hawk on wing

The hawk flew parallel to me as I walked back to my car. Then it made a sharp turn toward the left and looped around the canyon. I guess we can believe whatever we want, I thought. None of us that are still living actually know for sure what happens after death. I watched the hawk dive toward the water, soar up above the trees toward the heavens, then fly out of sight. As I took one more look at the natural beauty around me, I could not find the words to describe how I felt. Gram said that she would always be with me, and today, I chose to believe that she was right here.

"Thank you so much, Gram," I whispered.

Instantly, I saw the hawk fly overhead.

"You're welcome," the wind answered as it whistled through the bird's wings, and the canyon that surrounded me, echoed the same. Afterward, all was quiet.

I got back into the car, feeling ready to move ahead.

I drove out of the parking lot and headed farther north toward New England. At three in the afternoon, I pulled into the parking deck that was attached to the building where I worked. The sign pointing to the Boston Times led me up the steps, and to the twelfth floor, quite unnoticed.

This time of the day, people were usually heading home, or out somewhere covering a story. Few people were around. I unlocked my door, entered my office, and sat down behind my desk. I looked around and remembered how busy my life use to be here. How insane it was to always be embroiled in the headlines of today's stories that quickly ebbed into tomorrow's old news. There were the half truths, and the little lies that belonged to that way of life. I was on top. I thought I had all the answers. Half a lifetime went by, and I never expected the road to bend, or that I would hear the midnight chime.

Gram knew it was time. She knew that I had enough of the absurd, the caviar, and the delight. Gram yanked me back from the edge, and gave me a chance to see a different way of life. She held in front of me a vision of the humble and the sublime. Gram believed in something more lasting and, today, so did I.

I sat down at my desk, and swiveled the chair around to look out of the window. I gazed at the Boston skyline. I heard the noise of the city, and felt the rapid heartbeat of the people rushing from one place to another. I knew I had outlived this life, and I was ready, really ready, to move on to the next. I did not belong here anymore. Amazingly, I found myself longing for the simple more than the complex. I wanted to be less colorful and more black and white. I think we hold on to our feelings, our circumstances, and our attitudes long after they are relevant in our lives, I thought, and I immediately remembered Mr. Donald's words. 'Sometimes, Tess, we make the right decision after trying all the wrong ones. That may take awhile.'

"Hi Tess," a deep voice said. I turned my chair from the window, and saw Jim, my boss, standing in the doorway.

"I received your call, a few hours ago," he said, looking a little surprised.

"You're going to need to sit down, Jim," He pulled the chair up to my desk.

"I'm going to be leaving the newspaper, and taking up farming," I said very seriously. "Please, do not ask me any questions because I can't begin to explain. I promise I will write a book about it someday and send you the first copy. It will explain it all."

Jim, looking very surprised, respected my wishes, and only asked when I would be leaving.

"Today, Jim," I answered. Molly has been filling in for me, and she is doing a great job. Just let her continue, okay?"

"Okay, Tess. Just the other day, I had this unusual feeling that we would be standing here like this, and telling me that you were not coming back. It's almost like a dejavu.

I hate to see you go. You are one of the best in your field. You know if you ever want to come back, just give me a call, and the job is yours."

"Thanks Jim," I said.

He turned to leave, hesitated, and then turned back.

"Take good care of yourself, Tess, I know that you would not be doing this if you did not believe that it was what you truly wanted. By the way, I'll be anxiously waiting for that book."

He walked over to me, hugged me, and left my office.

I collected some personal things and the books I wanted, and I left the rest with a note for Molly. She always liked my office anyway. I pinned a letter on the main message board saying good bye and thanking everyone for their friendship and support throughout the years that I worked for the newspaper. I wished everyone well, and I closed by saying that I was well on my way to becoming an unreasonably happy woman. I took one more look around and headed for my car.

The drive home was one of those times where my mind kept drifting, and I was not able to carry through on any one thought. I was leaving this great city, my rewarding career, my immediate circle of friends, and heading off to live on my Gram's farm. This farm and small town was so far in my past, I could hardly remember what it was like. I was somewhat anxious, but convinced of the outcome. What happened to me was not imagined. Perhaps, if I ignored the signs, eventually, as the wheel of life turned faster, I would have another opportunity to change my way. However, Gram seemed as undaunted in death as she did in life, and I believe she wanted this for me now. She did not miss a beat. She quietly and insensibly worked whatever and whenever she could for me to take the path of least resistance. How imperfect our vision is from here. How perfect the view is from There.

"I'm headed home, Gram," I said out loud, feeling at peace with myself. I remembered her words on the day I graduated from the university. Before she left for home, we drank chocolate milkshakes at our favorite ice cream parlor, where we always ended our visits. 'You know Tess, you will not always know the right thing to do, but when you know, when you know what the right thing is, it will be difficult not to do it.'

Going back to Gram's today was easy. The road that took me away was now bringing me home.

Day Eleven

It was early morning. Like a candle that radiates light from the center of its flame, the dawn brightness glowed through the lace curtains and into Grams room. Full of enthusiasm and ready for the day, I made my way down the back steps to the kitchen. Today, I am just thankful, I thought. I perked some coffee and began to think about all the things I had to do. Finding a job, cleaning the house, mending the disrepair, and getting started with some new projects were all on on my list.

"There you go, Tess," I said out loud. "You are still living at a hectic pace in order to get things done. You may as well be in Boston, grabbing the cup of fast coffee and heading out to work. Gram didn't bring you home for that."

I somehow knew that out of the chaos of the past week, and my past life, a new order was emerging. I needed some time to adjust, and a lot of practice in this new way of life. With Gramps white mug filled with hot coffee in hand, Jake and I headed up the hill to the Springhouse for some solitude, some thinking, dreaming, and silent reflection.

It was quiet here this morning, and I was fascinated by the simplicity of it all. There were no trains loading, people rushing to work, or taxies being hailed. There were no corner newsstands opening for business, or street vendors preparing for the day. There were no time lines, horns honking, or the smell of breakfast foods from the sidewalk cafes. The only living things looking for something to eat were a few chipmunks, and some birds. Deer were starting to move around in the woods behind me. In the stillness of the morning air, there was only this silence that Gram described, beautiful silence, and in that silence, peace. No wonder Gram felt an urgency to pass this on to me. The transparent images, the persuasive voices, and the enthralling letters were nowhere to be found. I didn't need them anymore. I was ready to be part of all this. At the Springhouse, the journey would begin just like it did for Gram, I thought. 'Watch for the signs, Tess, and hope you don't miss them,' I remember Gram telling me. 'Pay attention and the answers will come. His timing is impeccable.'

About mid morning, I returned to the house. I was leaving to pick up Jake when I heard the approaching sound of tires crunching against the stone road. Luke thought of it first. Peaking out the parlor window, I saw him park the truck alongside the barn, open the door for Jake to jump out, and both of them headed toward the back door. I felt unusually nervous about seeing Luke today, perhaps because of the news I had to tell him.

"Good morning to both of you," I said, greeting them. As I pushed the screen door open, it made that old, creaky noise and gave me the reassurance that everything was as it should be in this moment. I was where I was supposed to be.

"Good morning, Tess, I hope you don't mind that I took the liberty of dropping Jake off, but I wanted to have some time to say good bye without being rushed at the clinic." Luke said.

"No, no, Luke, I'm glad you brought him home. Please come in and have a cup of coffee. I brought some delicious corn muffins from my favorite bakery while I was in Boston yesterday. I hope I could talk you into having one," I smiled.

"Boston? You went to Boston yesterday? I'm a little confused. May I ask why?" Luke looked puzzled.

"Oh, Luke, it's a long story, and I'm not even sure I believe it myself, but we would be here all day if I started from the beginning. I'm sure that your patients would not appreciate it if you do not show up for them today," I said.

I poured the coffee for both of us and brought the corn muffins to the table with some whipped butter on the side.

"Well, you are right, I do need to get to work today, so maybe you can share all this with me when you come back for a visit sometime. This coffee hits the spot and the muffins look delicious, Tess," Luke smiled as he tasted the corn muffin.

He looked down at Jake situated at his feet and patiently waiting for some crumbs to drop.

"Jake is in very good shape and all ready for his trip," Luke said, taking another bite of his muffin. "When will you be starting out for home?" he questioned.

Tess hesitated. She wanted to be absolutely sure that she was making the right decision before she said anything to Luke. This was not unusual. Gram knew that she was always hard to convince. Could she hope for another sign? I'll leave it in her hands, I thought.

At that moment, the grandfather clock in the parlor chimed twelve times. Tess glanced at the kitchen clock. The hands pointed to eleven forty-five. That was enough. Gram had come through for her again, perhaps for the last time.

Then Tess, with a reassuring smile on her face, took a deep breath and immediately blurted out,

"I am home, Luke."

Luke slowly lowered the coffee cup from his mouth and swallowed hard. Tilting his head with a slight nod, he began to smile, and then he began to smile more.

"Are you saying that you are coming back to Hopewell, Tess?"

"Yes, Luke. That is the reason I went to Boston yesterday. I talked to my boss and resigned my position on the newspaper. I made some plans and arrangements with a moving company and realtor, and here I am. There is much more to this final decision, but just let me say right now that even though Gram is gone, she has really pulled some strings this last week. I have decided to keep this farm and live here, and although I do not know where I am going with all this, I hope to know when I get there. Now if you will excuse me, I need to order a new tractor. The fields need some mowing and care, and I need to place a pot of rosemary near the back door for good luck."

"Tess," Luke said, as he got up from his chair, "I can't begin to read between the lines. I just want to say that I am delighted you will be staying here. If you need some help getting the farm in order, I would love to help you. I think we should celebrate. Would you like to go out for a celebration dinner next weekend after both of us have some time to get our arms around all of this? I mean all three of us," as he reached down to pet Jake on the head.

Luke was half way out the door, when he turned around and gave me a big hug.

"For some strange reason, I feel as if I have known you a long time," Luke said. "Who knows? Maybe I have."

Then the screen door gently creaked as he closed it behind him.

I felt strong. I felt happy. I felt at peace. Clearing the dishes from the table, there was a new sense of pride in the farm and in myself. I knew that there were still many moving pieces to this decision, but a new adventure was ahead for me. I was hoping that it would include an opportunity for me to give back for all that I received.

I felt blessed and honored to have been raised by Gram and Gramps on this beautiful piece of land, in this simple yet gracious place that I use to call, and will once again call, my home. Gram was right.

The world is full wonder, each time a new sun breaks
It leaves us with a story, as the moon and owl awake
The story is a message, for the open heart to take
The world is full wonder, each time a new sun breaks

The Field

Tess and her new Tractor

Twelve Months Later

Time passed very quickly on the farm. I had been home one year already, and each day I was more excited to be back. It was a balancing act with the chores and my jobs however there was one thing for sure, every day began in the early morning at the Springhouse.

When I lived in Boston, the months seemed to fly by. On the farm, it was remarkable to see the seasons change slowly as the old ebbed away, and the new began. Each spring, I began to look for the return of the robins looking for worms in the field. The smell of the musty mosses and the fertile earth replaced the ice and snow. The grass started to turn green, and daylight stayed around a little longer. When summer arrived, it brought with it warm, sunny days, and the promise of the returning perennials. The tomatoes swelled on the vines, and the fruit trees began to produce their fruits. Then the chill of autumn arrived. This was my favorite time of the year on the farm. There were the cool, crisp mornings that slipped into the warm, quiet afternoons, then quietly returned to the cool, crisp nights. It was nature's way of preparing for its long winter sleep. The corn stalks dried in the field, and along with the golden wheat, waited to be harvested. The geese flew in V-formation across the gray overcast sky, and disappeared behind the mountains of colorful leaves that fell to the ground after their impressive display. Winter turned the farm into a white wonderland. From the window, I watched the snowflakes fall, and the little puffs of snow collect on the dried cone flower heads.

I nestled into my comfortable chair by the open fire. Life moved me along with the beauty of each season, lifting me up into purer air, and then releasing me back on solid ground. I visited friends like Mrs. Como, Janice, Eunice, Mr. Donald and Louise almost weekly. It gave me a chance to

171

appreciate these fine people that passed through my day and touched my life.

After three months, I took a job at the Hopewell Chronicle. It was like coming home again. The circle was complete. This time, I was not doing odd jobs after school. This time I was their free lance writer covering the ordinary stories of the accomplishments of the extraordinary people of Hopewell, and the surrounding small towns.

I volunteered at the library, working under the supervision of my friend, Louise. I read stories to the children on Saturday mornings, returned books to their proper place on the book shelves, and organized reading and other events to benefit the town. No matter what the day brought for me to do at the library, I made sure it did not end without me walking past Gram's book and running my hand across her name. It was my time to celebrate her, and thank her for bringing me home.

One afternoon a week, I volunteered at the elementary school, helping children with their reading and writing skills. It amazed me to see how eager they were to satisfy their desire to learn. Many times, I became the student as these small teachers who, with their insatiable curiosity and their innocent deeds, gathered inspiration from the little aspects of life that I often took for granted.

I knew that I was in the right place at the right time, and if I were given the opportunity to it again, I would have been here a lot sooner.

The house was my first project. There was a lot to repair and restore, and at times my ability to do the work was lacking. I was careful not to change too much around the old house. I didn't want all the things level and perfect, for I was still drawn to the worn and weathered. I needed to fix the leak in the slate roof, but I didn't want to remove the squeak in the kitchen and parlor floorboards. I didn't want to silence the screen door, or the hundred other little noises that were part of this grand old house. I was afraid that if the crackling and clatter disappeared, so would the marvelous memories and warm pleasure that I wanted to keep alive there. In the end, I sought to keep the fragrant familiarity of this house along with the unique space and personal character that Gram had created. Her grace and charm when folks entered her home made them want to settle in and stay for a while.

In so many ways, this farm changed me, more than I have changed the farm.

As for Luke, I had no idea the depths of his devotion to me. Our paths, which had crossed for a reason, blossomed into a relationship that was beautiful and lasting. We worked the farm together. During those busy days, he would put his arms around me when I least expected it, and I would kiss him gently in return. I learned lessons from him that will last me the rest of my life. I feel honored and blessed to know him.

We spent days together in the old hotel in Herron, and visited the canyon often. We watched the mountains change from lush green in the spring and summer to a vibrant mix of reds, oranges, and yellows during the fall, and finally to a brilliant white in the winter.

It was a beautiful year, but ended quite unexpectedly for me. In late November, as the overcast day began to sink into the western sky, Luke and I headed for the Springhouse and the honeymoon hideout with the wooden box of Grams ashes. We decided that it was time for us to carry out Grams wishes. Luke and I opened the box and spread her ashes around her bench by the Springhouse. There was a profound silence between us that matched the stillness around us.

Then Luke turned to me.

"You know Tess, when I stand here with you, I realize that one lifetime will not be enough for us," Luke said.

There was a certain warmth in being close and quiet. During this whole year, Luke and I found inspiration in our love, and the love of living the lives that we were meant to live.

"I feel the same way, Luke," Tess said.

Luke took her hand in his, and they walked a few feet over to the honeymoon hideout. He looked at her with the same gentle look that he gave her when they first met in the canyon. Through their time together, that look had turned into adoration for her, and she returned the love by her admiration for him.

"You know I've learned that it is not what you have in your life, Tess, but who you have in your life that counts," Luke said, smiling at her. "I love you, and I want to marry you. I want to embrace you forever."

He - the land, the wind, and the sea,
whispers
"Will you marry me?"
She – the moon, the stars, and the sky
answers
"Yes"

The Wedding

The following October, the wedding took place at the Springhouse. It was a plain and simple ceremony. It was the celebration of just a man loving and embracing just a woman for just a time. Luke looked so handsome in his black suit and white shirt. I wore a mauve tea dress with Gram's pearls around my neck, and an ivory straw hat that had a crimson rose and a thin millinery veil attached to the silk band. I wore my diamond ring and matching wedding band on my left hand.

We invited some dear friends that knew us and Gram, and the minister that held Grams funeral rite married us at four in the afternoon. He had a short sermon about loving each other, and ended the ceremony by quoting a saying from an old proverb.

"Someday, after we have mastered the wind, tides, and gravity," he said, "we will then harness the energies of love. Then for the second time in the history of the world, man will have created fire."

After the wedding we all gathered around a long table set in a clearing by the honeymoon hideout. We were surrounded by beautiful trees with their colorful fall leaves. Everyone enjoyed some bacon-corn chowder specially prepared by Mrs. Como. Mr. Donald served a delicious ham and chicken dinner accompanied by a butternut bake. Fresh apple cake with cream, and coffee was served for dessert. There was plenty of conversation among our friends, and heartfelt congratulations for us.

As the last light of the day was draining from the sky, and the shadows were spreading out from under the trees, our guests began to leave. Mrs. Como was the last to go, and Luke took her arm and carefully escorted her down the hill to her car that was parked next to the house.

I sat on Grams chair waiting for Luke to return. Staring at the honeymoon hideout, I just imagined the joy that Gram and Gramps experienced after they married and lived on this farm.

How I wished that both of them could have been here today to celebrate with Luke and me. I pictured them standing in the honeymoon hideout and watching the ceremony through the small curtained window that faced the Springhouse. I imagined conversation going on between them. They were probably bragging about their delight in opening my heart to a greater good, the love of Luke and, of course, bringing me home.

At that moment, reality replaced imagination. A light flickered in the window of the honeymoon hideout, and I caught a glimpse of two shadows holding a lantern. The shadows turned into images with the exact likeness of Gram and Gramps. They were standing together inside and looking out the open window of the honeymoon hut. As I moved closer, they did not seem to notice me, or pay any attention to me if they did. Instead, they continued talking with each other. Gramps had his arm around Gram, and she was smiling and looking into his eyes. Their voices were elated and playful, and, yes, they were talking about me.

"What do you think Gramps?" I heard Gram say.

"Well, I think it is a hard job to give a woman back her true meaning in life," he said, "but you made it happen, Gram. You really did it. Your love for her, and your determination influenced our Tess. You must be very proud of yourself, Gram."

He kissed her gently on the cheek. Gram seemed to glow with pride. Gramps continued.

"Now, with that all taken care of Gram, what do you say we get a cold drink of water from our Springhouse before we head back to our Real Home, where we belong.

Bewildered, I watched their images fade. I rubbed my eyes, hoping to see them again, but all that remained was a reflection of the last ray of sunshine coming through the trees and resting on the closed and empty window.

Honeymoon Hut

Luke returned and took my hand, and together we started to walk back to the house. I paused when I felt a gentle breeze move past me, followed by another quick breeze right behind it. Then the scent of Chantilly and Prince Albert tobacco drifted by. I turned around just in time to see the door to the Springhouse fly open, hesitate, and then slam shut. The click of the lock followed immediately behind it.

I turned toward Luke, nodded my head, and smiled proudly. Unaware of the moment's happenings, he smiled back lovingly.

"Good bye, Gram. Good bye, Gramps," I whispered, "until we see each other again."

Epilogue

Many months and years have passed, and I am now in my early eighties. Luke and I are still holding hands and doing the best we can to run the farm. He gave up his veterinary practice five years ago, but still comes home with some strays, or makes house calls to the neighboring farms that need his help. He will die with his deep caring and ardent dedication to the service of animals.

As for me, I faithfully visit the Springhouse every morning. I need a cane to get there now, but I insist on going, and I insist on doing it alone. There are no more obscure images or specters there to greet me anymore, but I continue to feel Grams spirit as I sit on her bench and look toward the Springhouse. Her voice was stronger and louder in the past because I could not understand it as well, but now the voice is softer and more subtle for I listen with an open heart instead of human ears.

I no longer think about the great beating heart of the city that once forced the life energy into my day. I no longer need the unexpected apparitions of the past to display their magic. I just sit by the Springhouse, in the woods, on my farm, and that is enough for me.

A journalist at heart, I wrote a book about my journey. In the beginning, there was a part of me that felt my experience was too unbelievable to tell anyone, but as the words began to emerge from my mind and unto paper, I realized that my journey was not unique at all. I did not own this story, for it is written by someone, in some form, every day. I am one of many that was offered an opportunity to step off the path of self interest and self seeking and cut a new path. I was offered the challenge to live each moment instead of living years ahead of each day. So far, I am confident that I have made the right choice.

Every year that I live, I am convinced that the spirit of change moves among us in some form every moment. I also know that the catalyst for that change may not always be as mysterious and dramatic as mine. However, it is that human being, who has altered their life in the absence of the spectacular and the astounding, that is the true recipient of **The Gift** far greater than mine.

The world is full wonder, each time a new sun breaks
It leaves us with a story, as the moon and owl awake
The story is a message, for the open heart to take
The world is full wonder, each time a new sun breaks

Tess

Made in the USA
Middletown, DE
13 July 2025

10569381R00108